I0720994

Second Chances

A Josefina Classic
Volume 2

by Valerie Tripp

⭐ American Girl®

Published by American Girl Publishing
Copyright © 1998, 2000, 2014 American Girl

All rights reserved. No part of this book may be used or reproduced
in any manner whatsoever without written permission except in the case
of brief quotations embodied in critical articles and reviews.

Questions or comments? Call 1-800-845-0005,
visit **americangirl.com**, or write to Customer Service,
American Girl, 8400 Fairway Place, Middleton, WI 53562.

Printed in China
15 16 17 18 19 20 21 LEO 10 9 8 7 6 5 4 3 2

All American Girl marks, BeForever™, Josefina®,
and Josefina Montoya® are trademarks of American Girl.

Grateful acknowledgment is made to Enrique R. Lamadrid for permission
to reprint the verse on p. 49, adapted from "*Versos a la madre/*Verses to Mother"
in *Tesoros del Espíritu: A portrait in sound of Hispanic New Mexico,* University of
New Mexico, University of New Mexico Press, © 1994 Enrique R. Lamadrid.

This book is a work of fiction. Any similarity to real persons, living or dead,
is coincidental and not intended by American Girl. References to real events,
people, or places are used fictitiously. Other names, characters, places, and
incidents are the products of imagination.

Cover image by Michael Dwornik and Juliana Kolesova

Cataloging-in-Publication Data available from the Library of Congress

To Peggy Jackson,
with thanks

To Kathy Borkowski,
Val Hodgson, Peg Ross,
Jane Varda, and Judy Woodburn,
with thanks

To Rosalinda Barrera, Juan García,
Sandra Jaramillo, Skip Keith Miller,
Felipe Mirabal, Tey Diana Rebolledo,
Orlando Romero, and Marc Simmons,
with thanks

Beforever™

The adventurous characters you'll meet in
the BeForever books will spark your curiosity
about the past, inspire you to find your voice
in the present, and excite you about your future.
You'll make friends with these girls as you share
their fun and their challenges. Like you, they are
bright and brave, imaginative and energetic,
creative and kind. Just as you are, they are
discovering what really matters: Helping others.
Being a true friend. Protecting the earth.
Standing up for what's right. Read their stories,
explore their worlds, join their adventures.
Your friendship with them will BeForever.

TABLE *of* CONTENTS

Josefina and her family speak Spanish, so you'll
see some Spanish words in this book. You'll find
the meanings and pronunciations of these words
in the glossary on page 158.

Remember that in Spanish, "j" is pronounced
like "h." That means Josefina's name is
pronounced "ho-seh-FEE-nah."

Spring Sprouts

osefina loved spring. She loved the way it came swooping in like a bird on a breeze. She loved the way it woke the earth up from its deep winter sleep and made the *rancho* a busy, lively place. Baby animals were born in the spring. The sun stayed longer in the sky, and there were small green surprises here and there where things were beginning to grow.

Just now, Josefina had a surprise to share. She swung open the door to the weaving room and poked her head inside. "Tía Dolores!" she said eagerly. "Please, come with me. I have something wonderful to show you."

Tía Dolores looked up. The wind through the open door fluttered the pages of her ledger book, which was on her lap. Josefina saw that Papá was in the weaving room, too. He was counting finished woven blankets, and Tía Dolores was writing the numbers in her ledger with her quill pen.

"Oh! Forgive me for interrupting, Papá," said Josefina.

"Well," said Papá cheerfully. "I'd like to see something wonderful, too. I suppose our counting can wait, don't you, Dolores?"

"Of course!" said Tía Dolores, putting down her pen.

Papá made a little bow from the waist and held out his hand toward the door. Tía Dolores swept by him, and they both followed Josefina as she walked quickly across the courtyard to the back corner.

"Just look!" said Josefina. She knelt down and lifted a handful of dead leaves. Underneath, skinny yellow-green sprouts were sticking up out of the soil. Josefina lifted another handful of leaves, and then another, and every time there were green shoots underneath. "Sprouts everywhere!" she said. "More than ever before! Pretty soon the whole corner will be full of flowers."

"*Sí*, it will," agreed Papá. He sounded pleased. He put his hand on Josefina's head and smoothed her hair.

Tía Dolores knelt down, too. Josefina loved the way her aunt never minded getting dirt on her skirt or her hands. The sun shone on Tía Dolores's dark red hair as she bent over the sprouts. Josefina knew Tía Dolores was pleased, too. These sprouts were a promise kept.

Josefina's mamá had planted the flowers in this corner. During the year after Mamá died, Josefina had cared for the flowers as well as she could. Then last fall, Florecita, the meanest goat on the rancho, had torn up the flowers and eaten every last one. Josefina had thought Mamá's flowers would never grow again. But Tía Dolores had promised that they'd be all right. Now she turned and smiled at Josefina. "Didn't I tell you?" she said. "Flowers with roots as deep as these can survive a lot—even a visit from Florecita!"

Josefina grinned. "I'm still going to keep Florecita away from them!" she said.

"Don't worry," said Papá. "Florecita will be too busy to bother your flowers this spring. She's going to have a baby very soon."

"Oh, no!" said Josefina, pretending to groan. "I hope Florecita's baby isn't like her. I don't think I could stand two horrible goats trying to bully me!" Josefina

laughed along with Papá and Tía Dolores. She used
to be afraid of Florecita. She wasn't the least little bit
afraid of the goat anymore, but she didn't like her the
least little bit, either.

It was cool that night. Josefina was glad she had
left a blanket of dead leaves spread over the sprouts to
protect them. And she was glad she had a blanket of
woven wool spread over her lap, though the family *sala*
was warm.

Josefina and her sisters, Ana, Francisca, and Clara,
were sewing blankets. Woven material came off the
loom in narrow strips, which had to be sewn together
to make one wide blanket. Josefina made her stitches
strong and straight. All the sisters were good at sewing
blankets. They'd sewn many since the fall.

Tía Dolores was adding numbers in her ledger.
After a while, she paused and asked, "Josefina, your
birthday is coming soon, isn't it?"

"Sí," said Josefina. "I was born on March nine-
teenth, the feast of San José."

"When Mamá was alive, we always had a

celebration," said Francisca. She was Josefina's second oldest sister, and she loved parties.

"Well, I think we should have one this year, too," said Tía Dolores.

The sisters looked up, delighted.

"After all, we'll have several things to celebrate," Tía Dolores went on. "It's the feast of San José. Josefina will be ten. Spring will be here. And . . ." Tía Dolores smiled as she said, "God willing, we should have quite a lot of new sheep by then. I've added the figures. We've made sixty blankets. That's enough to trade for ninety sheep—forty-five ewes and forty-five lambs."

"That *is* good news!" exclaimed Josefina. She and Francisca both put their sewing aside and went to look over Tía Dolores's shoulder at her ledger. Ana, the oldest sister, murmured a prayer of thanks. Clara, who was next to Josefina in age, calmly continued to sew.

"It's good," said Clara. "But it doesn't mean we can stop making blankets. We'll need them to trade for *more* sheep."

"Oh, baa, baa, baa," Francisca bleated at Clara. "Don't be so tiresome! We all know that ninety sheep aren't enough to replace the hundreds that Papá lost in the flood last fall. But it's a good start! I think we should be very proud of ourselves. Sixty blankets is a lot. I know I worked hard on them."

Ana, Clara, and Josefina glanced at each other and then burst out laughing. Francisca complained more than anyone else about working on the blankets. Now she made it sound as if she'd been responsible for them all!

At first, Francisca scowled at her sisters' laughter. But in a moment she was laughing at herself along with them. "All right, all right," she admitted grudgingly. "The rest of you worked hard, too."

"We might not have *any* blankets to trade if it weren't for Tía Dolores," said Josefina. "It was her idea to turn blankets into sheep."

All the sisters nodded and looked at their aunt with fondness. After the terrible loss of the sheep, Tía Dolores had suggested that she and the sisters and other workers on the rancho weave the wool they already had into blankets and trade them for sheep. Now, just when spring lambs were being born, they had sixty blankets to turn into sheep!

"Papá will be pleased," said Ana.

"When do you think he'll go to the *pueblo* village to trade the blankets for Esteban Durán's sheep?" asked Josefina. Esteban, Papá's great friend, was a Pueblo Indian.

"Soon," said Tía Dolores. She smiled over her shoulder at Josefina. "Maybe you'd like to go with him." Tía Dolores knew that Josefina loved to go to the pueblo and see her friend Mariana, who was Esteban's granddaughter.

"May I find Papá right now and ask him?" Josefina said.

"Sí," said Tía Dolores, who always understood Josefina's eagerness. "Go. Wrap your *rebozo* around you. It's chilly."

"*Gracias!*" said Josefina. She gave Tía Dolores a quick hug and pulled her rebozo up over her head. She was just about to hurry out the door when an idea stopped her. "Tía Dolores," she said. "Won't you come with me? You should be the one to tell Papá about the blankets and the sheep."

Tía Dolores started to say no, but Ana and Francisca chimed together, saying, "Go on. It *is* your news to tell."

"Very well," laughed Tía Dolores. She put her sewing aside and took Josefina's hand, and together they went out into the cool spring night.

They found Papá in the goats' pen. He was sitting next to one of the goats with a lantern at his side. He glanced up when they came in, but he didn't say anything.

"Papá," Josefina began excitedly. "Tía Dolores has good news for . . ." Josefina stopped. She realized that the goat next to Papá was Florecita. But she had never seen Florecita like this. The goat was lying on her side, hardly breathing. Her eyes were shut. "Papá," asked Josefina, "what's wrong?"

"Florecita had her baby tonight," said Papá. "But she's too weak to nurse it. I don't think she'll live."

Josefina looked down at her old enemy, Florecita. Living on a rancho, Josefina had seen many animals die. She knew better than to think of the animals as anything more than useful and valuable property. Still, as she looked at Florecita—the goat who had bullied her and poked her and torn up Mamá's flowers— somehow she just couldn't help feeling sorry. "Can't we do anything?" she asked Papá.

"I don't think so," said Papá.

Josefina let go of Tía Dolores's hand and knelt
next to Papá. She stroked Florecita's side, but the goat
didn't move or open her eyes. Her breathing grew
slower and slower until at last it stopped. Florecita
was dead.

Josefina sighed. "Poor Florecita," she said softly.
Then she remembered something important. She
turned to Papá. "Where is Florecita's baby?" she asked.

Papá lifted the front corner of his *sarape*. Cradled
in his arm was a tiny goat.

"Oh!" gasped Josefina, pulling in her breath. Tía
Dolores gasped, too, and sank down on her knees
behind Josefina.

Very gently, Josefina reached out and touched the
goat's silky little ear. The goat turned her head and
nuzzled the palm of Josefina's hand. "Oh," Josefina
said again. The goat opened her eyes and Josefina
had to smile, because her yellow eyes looked just like
Florecita's, but without the evil glint. Suddenly, Josefina
knew what she must do. "Please, Papá," she asked.
"May I take care of Florecita's baby?"

Papá's kind face was full of concern. "The baby is

very weak, Josefina," he said. "It isn't easy to care for an animal this needy. I think you might be too young for the responsibility."

"I'm almost ten!" said Josefina. "Please let me try."

Still Papá hesitated. "You must realize . . ." he began. Then he stopped.

Tía Dolores put her arm around Josefina's shoulder. Then, in a gesture so swift Josefina thought she must have imagined it, Tía Dolores touched Papá's hand. Papá looked up at Tía Dolores, and Josefina saw that his eyes had a question in them. Tía Dolores nodded. She seemed to know what Papá had started to say, and she was encouraging him to say it.

Papá spoke slowly. "You must realize that there's a good chance the baby won't live, even if you do care for her," he said to Josefina. "Think how you'll feel if you become fond of the little goat and then she dies."

Josefina understood. Papá was afraid her heart would be broken as it had been when Mamá died. And for a moment, Josefina was afraid, too. But then she looked at the little goat and all her doubts fell away. "I have to try to save Florecita's baby, Papá," she said. "When any of God's creatures is sick or weak we have to try to make it better, don't we?" She held out her arms for the goat. "Please, Papá," she said.

Papá sighed. Carefully, he put the baby goat into Josefina's arms. She held the soft warm body nestled close to her chest and rubbed her cheek against the goat's fur. The baby goat gave one small bleat, closed her eyes, and went to sleep as if Josefina's arms were the safest place in the world.

"Take her back to the house," said Papá, "and keep her next to the fire. I'll bring some milk. She's too weak to nurse from one of the other goats. You'll have to teach her to drink." He stood up and looked at Josefina holding the helpless, sleeping goat. "She's yours to care for now."

"I'll take good care of her," said Josefina. "I promise."

"That's *Florecita's* baby?" Francisca asked. "She's such a sweet little thing!"

"*Very* little," said Clara. "Puny, really. It's going to be a lot of work and worry to make *that* goat healthy and strong."

"The poor motherless baby!" said Ana tenderly.

Josefina's sisters were gathered around her, staring at the baby goat, which was now awake in her arms. Tía Dolores poured the milk Papá brought into a bowl and placed it on the hearth. But when Josefina put the goat next to the milk, the little animal didn't seem to know what to do.

"Here," said Josefina. She dipped her fingers in the milk and then held them up to the goat's mouth. At first, the goat seemed too weak even to open her mouth. But then she sucked the milk off Josefina's fingers. "That's it," said Josefina. "That's the way."

Patiently, Josefina dipped her fingers in the milk again and again, feeding the little goat almost drop by drop. Josefina liked the tickling feeling of the goat's rough tongue on her fingers. She was sorry when the goat fell asleep again, before the milk bowl was empty.

"Clara's right. Taking care of that goat will be hard," said Francisca. "But I hope she grows up to be as big as Florecita, just not as mean."

"So do I," said Josefina, hugging the goat. "So do I."

That night, Josefina and the baby goat slept on a

wide bunk above the kitchen hearth called the shepherd's bed. Shepherds sometimes brought orphaned lambs there to sleep because it was heated by the hearth fire through the night. The little goat slept curved like a cat, her legs tucked under her body, her bony head resting on Josefina's hand. Josefina woke up often during the night. She wanted to be sure she could feel the little goat's heart beating and the warmth of its soft breath on her hand.

The little goat made it through the night. Before dawn the next morning, Papá brought Josefina a pouch filled with goat's milk. He attached a rag to the end of the pouch. Josefina held it to the baby goat's mouth. After licking it once or twice, the goat sucked on the rag and hungrily drank the milk out of the pouch.

"Look, Papá!" said Josefina. "Isn't she clever?"

"Sí," said Papá. He stroked the goat's head with the back of his finger.

Josefina thought the goat was *very* clever to have figured out how to drink from the pouch. In fact, Josefina believed that Florecita's baby was a superior animal in every way—even if she *was* rather small.

The baby goat grew stronger as each bright spring day passed. She seemed to thrive on warm sunshine, warm milk, and Josefina's warm affection. It was not long before the goat was following Josefina around everywhere on her quick, sturdy little legs.

"She's just like your shadow!" joked Tía Dolores. And so they all began to call the goat Sombrita, which means "little shadow."

Soon everyone was used to seeing Josefina and Sombrita together all over the rancho. Sombrita trip-trotted down to the stream every morning when Josefina went to fetch water for the household. Sombrita tagged along while Josefina fed the chickens, which made the chickens cluck and fuss. The little goat chased Josefina's broom as if it were a toy and sweeping were a game she and Josefina played with it. She dozed peacefully while Josefina worked at the loom, and bleated noisily while Josefina had a piano lesson with Tía Dolores. Josefina loved to look down and see Sombrita's cheerful face raised toward her hoping for a quick pat, a hug, or a scratch behind one floppy ear.

As Sombrita grew more frisky, Josefina had to keep an eye on her all the time. The rancho was a dangerous place for such a small creature. She might be kicked by a mule or stepped on by an ox. Josefina especially worried about snakes. Snakes were just awakening from their winter hibernation, so they were hungry. In the spring, a rattlesnake was quite likely to strike a baby animal like Sombrita and kill her. Josefina kept Sombrita close by, safe from harm. She had promised to take good care of the little goat, and it was a promise she intended to keep.

Tía Magdalena

O ne warm day, Tía Dolores, Josefina, and the sisters were planting seeds in the garden. Josefina used a sharp stick to make a hole in the earth. She dropped a seed in the hole, covered it with dirt, then patted the dirt in place. Josefina always liked to give the dirt an extra little pat, to encourage the seed to grow. Josefina and her sisters tended their garden with care. During the summer they'd carry water up from the stream every day to keep the earth moist. They'd pull weeds and shoo away pests. Then in the fall they'd harvest squash, beans, chiles, pumpkins, and melons.

"Oh, I'd love a big slice of melon right now!" said Francisca.

"Me, too," agreed Josefina. She sat back on her heels for a rest. The earth was cool beneath her knees, but the sun was hot on her shoulders.

"You'll have to wait until the end of the summer,"
said Clara. "We ate all our melons months ago."

"We were lucky to save as many as we did," said
Ana. The same storm that had killed Papá's sheep had
flooded the kitchen garden.

"We'll harvest all we plant today, God willing!"
said Tía Dolores. She nodded toward Sombrita, who
was bleating at the birds flying low near the garden.
"Fierce Sombrita is scaring away all the birds trying
to steal the seeds."

The sisters laughed, because the bold birds weren't
the least bit frightened by Sombrita. The goat saw that
she was the center of attention. She began to show off
by kicking up her heels and bleating even louder.

"Who is that noisy animal?" someone asked. It was
Tía Magdalena, walking through the gate. She was
Papá's older sister, who lived in the village.

The girls and Tía Dolores greeted her politely. Then
Tía Dolores answered her question. "That's Sombrita,"
she said. Her voice was full of fondness and pride as
she went on to say, "Josefina has cared for her since she
was born. The mother died."

"We all thought Sombrita would die, too," said Clara, who was always matter-of-fact. "She was so weak and pitiful."

Tía Magdalena looked interested. She bent down and scooped up Sombrita. She stroked the little goat gently, and Sombrita settled calmly in her arms. Then Tía Magdalena looked at Josefina. Her soft brown eyes were warm. "Why did you decide to take care of Sombrita?" she asked.

Josefina didn't know what to say. "I . . . I didn't stop to think about it," she said honestly. "I just . . . I had to, that's all."

"Has it been hard work?" asked Tía Magdalena.

"Oh, no!" said Josefina. "I love taking care of Sombrita!"

"You have done a good job of it," said Tía Magdalena. She handed Sombrita to Josefina. "Sombrita is a fine, healthy goat."

"Gracias, Tía Magdalena," said Josefina. She was pleased to be praised by her aunt. Tía Magdalena was an important person in her family, especially to Josefina, because she was Josefina's godmother. She was an important, respected person in the village, too.

Tía Magdalena was the healer, or *curandera*. She knew more about healing than anyone else. People who were injured or ill went to her for care, and she always knew just what to do.

Now Tía Magdalena turned to Tía Dolores. "Here are the mustard leaves you asked for," she said. "Tell your cook Carmen to brew tea from them and give it to her husband Miguel to drink if his stomach ache comes back."

"Gracias," said Tía Dolores, taking the leaves.

"Please tell her not to use it all at once," said Tía Magdalena. "I haven't many leaves left. Tansy mustard is usually blooming everywhere by now, but I haven't been able to find any yet this year."

"I've seen some growing by the stream," Josefina piped up.

"Your young eyes are better than my old ones!" said Tía Magdalena. "Perhaps you'll gather some leaves for me." Tía Magdalena tilted her head and looked at Josefina as if she were considering something. "And perhaps when you bring the leaves, you can stay for a while and help me. My storeroom needs a spring cleaning."

"Oh, I'd like that very much!" said Josefina.

"Good!" said Tía Magdalena. She smiled, and Josefina blushed with pride and pleasure. How nice to have pleased Tía Magdalena!

The very next day Josefina skipped along the road to the village under a clean blue sky. She had a bunch of tansy mustard leaves in her hand for Tía Magdalena. Papá, Tía Dolores, and the sisters were going to the village, too. Josefina had left Sombrita behind under Carmen's watchful eye. Josefina missed Sombrita, but she knew the little goat would only be in the way today. In the morning, the men and boys were going to clean out the water ditches, called *acequias,* while the women and girls replastered the church. And in the afternoon, Josefina would be too busy to keep an eye on Sombrita when she went to help Tía Magdalena.

Most of the villagers had already gathered in the *plaza* at the center of the village when Papá and his family arrived. They called out greetings. *"Buenos días!"* they said.

"Buenos días," Papá replied. "It's a fine day to work, by God's grace."

"It is," said Señor Sánchez, who was in charge of the water ditches. "Let's begin." He and Papá and the other men shouldered their tools and set off to work. Clearing the acequias was a very important springtime job. Later in the spring, when the snow on the mountaintops melted, the acequias had to be clear of leaves and sticks and weeds so that the water could flow to the fields. Without water, nothing planted that spring would grow.

"We'd better begin our work, too," said Señora Sánchez. The women and girls agreed. They took off their shoes, rolled up their sleeves, covered their hair, and tucked up their skirts. Replastering the church was another important chore. It was normally done later in the spring. But the weather had been so unusually warm the past few weeks, the women were replastering much earlier this year. Josefina was glad. As she scooped up a handful of gritty mud plaster, she decided replastering was a chore that was fun.

"Watch out!" Josefina shouted at Clara, who stood between her and the church. Clara ducked down, and

Josefina flung her handful of mud plaster at the wall of the church, where it stuck—*splat*—in a glob.

Clara laughed, saying, "You'll splatter mud all over if you do it that way." Clara was neat. She *pressed* her handful of mud plaster against the wall.

But even Clara was easygoing today, thought Josefina as she spread the glob of mud over the *adobe* bricks so that it was smooth and even. The women and girls gossiped and chattered as they worked. The very oldest ladies sat in the shade, keeping an eye on the babies. They called out jokes and encouragement to the others. Every once in a while someone would start a song and everyone would join in. Voices high and low, in tune and out of tune, rose up from all around the church.

Josefina liked making the church walls whole again. Later, she and some other children climbed up onto the roof to spread a new layer of mud plaster on it as well. Josefina loved the feeling of the mud oozing between her bare toes. It was exhilarating to be up high, closer to the huge white clouds and the brilliant blue sky. Josefina and the others shrieked with joy as they slipped and slid on the slick mud to tamp it flat.

"Josefina!" Clara called out. She was standing below on the ground, looking up, shading her eyes with her hand. "Tuck your skirt up higher in the back or you'll get mud on it and look messy at Tía Magdalena's this afternoon."

"And pull up your rebozo so that it shades your face," Francisca added. "Your nose is getting as red as a tomato."

Josefina looked down at tidy, sensible Clara and at beautiful Francisca, who was fussy about her skin. She knew that right now her sisters envied her. *They* were too old to be on the roof.

Almost ten is a wonderful age to be, thought Josefina, exuberantly slooshing her feet through the mud. *I'm not too old to slip and slide on the roof, and yet I am old enough to take care of Sombrita and old enough to help Tía Magdalena!* She waved to her sisters and cheerfully ignored their advice.

"Bless you, child!" said Tía Magdalena that afternoon when she saw Josefina at her door with the bouquet of mustard leaves. "Come in!"

"Gracias," said Josefina. She stepped inside and took a deep breath. Nowhere else on earth smelled quite the way Tía Magdalena's house smelled. It reminded Josefina of the way the corner of the back courtyard smelled when the sun shone strong on Mamá's flowers. But mixed in with the scent of flowers was the sharp, nose-tickling scent of spices and the musty, earthy tang of the herbs that hung upside down in bunches from the beams.

Tía Magdalena smiled when she saw Josefina looking up at the herbs. "You'd like to know how to use them, wouldn't you?" she asked.

Josefina nodded, wondering how Tía Magdalena had known.

"The mint leaves ease stomach aches. The pennyroyal brings a fever down. I use the *manzanilla* flowers to make a tea to cure a baby's colic," Tía Magdalena said, pointing to each herb as she named it. "And speaking of babies, how is your sweet Sombrita today?"

"She's *very* well, thank you," answered Josefina, grinning.

"She's *very* fortunate to have you caring for her!" said Tía Magdalena. Her face looked merry. Tía

Magdalena was much older than Papá. Her gray hair was streaked with white. But when she smiled as she did now, her expression was lively. And when she moved, her step was quick and light. "Now, we must do some work," she said. "Come with me."

Tía Magdalena led Josefina to the small storeroom at the back of her house. The ceiling was low and there was only one narrow window. But the room looked bright because the walls were whitewashed a snowy white and the wooden table and door frames were polished until the wood was a shiny yellow. More herbs hung from the beams in this room. Along one wall there were shelves lined with jars of all shapes and sizes.

Tía Magdalena tilted her head toward the jars. "Here's where I need your help," she said to Josefina. Her eyes sparkled. "Why don't we make a game of it? You lift a jar down from the shelf, look inside, and see if you can guess what's in it. I'll dust the jar, you dust the shelf, and then you can put the jar back. All right?"

"Sí!" said Josefina. She reached for the biggest, most important-looking jar of all. It was blue-and-white china.

"Oh, not that jar!" said Tía Magdalena. "It's empty."

"It looks very old," said Josefina.

"Indeed it is," said Tía Magdalena. "It's probably the oldest thing in this house. It's even older than I am!" she joked. "It's an apothecary jar. I don't know how it came to be in our village, but I know that it's been here for more than a hundred years. The woman who was curandera before I was gave it to me. She got it from the woman who was curandera before her. Long ago, I believe, there was a whole set of jars like it. That's the only one left." Tía Magdalena pointed to a smaller jar next to the blue-and-white one. "Let's start with that jar instead," she said.

Josefina took the smaller jar off the shelf and looked inside. "It looks like pumpkin stems," she said. "Could it be?"

"Sí," said Tía Magdalena. "You're sharp to recognize them." She dusted the jar as Josefina dusted the shelf. "There's nothing in the world better for a sore throat," she said. "You toast the pumpkin stem, grind it to a powder, mix it with fat and salt, and rub it on the throat inside and out."

Josefina wrinkled her nose when she smelled the

inside of the next jar. "I think it's bear grease," she said.

"Right again," said Tía Magdalena. "You mix it with onions and rub it on a person's chest to ease congestion."

The next jar Josefina opened made her sneeze. "Oh, that must be *inmortal*," said Tía Magdalena, chuckling. "It makes you sneeze and sneeze and sneeze. The more you sneeze, the sooner your cold is gone."

Josefina enjoyed helping Tía Magdalena. Every jar had a story in it, because every jar held something that Tía Magdalena used as a remedy. There was dried deer blood to be mixed with water and drunk for strength. There was vinegar that was so strong it made Josefina's eyes water. It was used as a soak to stop infections. In another jar there was a terrible-smelling herb that was used to soothe achy joints. Josefina guessed what was in most of the jars. But once she came to something she didn't recognize.

"I don't know what this is," she told Tía Magdalena.

"That's the root of a globe mallow plant," said Tía Magdalena. "I crush it and make a paste to put on a rattlesnake bite to draw out the poisonous venom."

She handed one of the roots to Josefina. "Put that in
your pouch and take it home with you," she said with
a mischievous look. "And someday, ask your papá if
he recognizes it."

"Papá?" asked Josefina.

"Sí," said Tía Magdalena. "Once, when he was a
boy just about your age, he was guarding the sheep.
He tried to scare away a rattlesnake by hitting it with
a pebble from his sling. He missed. The snake got mad
and bit him. Your papá killed the snake with a rock
before he came to me for help. That was very brave,
but very foolish of him! If you don't get the venom out
right away, it can kill you." She shook her head. "I'll
never forget the sight of him coming toward me, so
proud of his own courage, and with that dead snake
slung over his shoulders!"

Josefina put the root in her pouch and shuddered.
She hated even *hearing* about snakes! But she liked to
hear Tía Magdalena tell stories about Papá when he
was a boy.

"Your papá was always too fearless and too stubborn for his own good," Tía Magdalena said as she
dusted a jar. "And too quiet. But that didn't matter

when your mamá was alive. She knew what he was thinking anyway."

Josefina was surprised at how easy it was to talk to Tía Magdalena about Mamá as they worked. "Sometimes it seems so long ago that Mamá died," Josefina said. "Sometimes it seems like it just happened. And sometimes I'll see Mamá in a dream, and it seems as if she's still with us."

"Sí," said Tía Magdalena. Her old brown eyes seemed to see right into Josefina's heart. "That is how it is always going to be for you."

"Sí," said Josefina, running her cloth over a shelf to dust it. "And for Papá, too, I think. He's not quite so quiet and sad as he was just after Mamá died. It has been better for us all since Tía Dolores came. We needed her."

"Well," said Tía Magdalena, handing a jar to Josefina. "Perhaps *she* needed *you*, too."

Josefina wondered what Tía Magdalena meant. But just then, Tía Magdalena said, "I think it's time for a cup of tea, don't you?" And so Josefina didn't have a chance to ask.

Second Chances

hen they were seated with their tea and some sweet cookies, Tía Magdalena said, "You've done well today."

"Gracias," said Josefina. "I was glad to help." She sipped her hot mint tea and gathered her courage to say what she was thinking. "I've really enjoyed all of this afternoon," she said. "And I was thinking . . . I was thinking that I'd like to be a curandera when I am older."

Tía Magdalena studied Josefina's face as she listened.

Josefina was encouraged. "Do you think you could teach me?" she asked. "When I'm old enough, I mean. I know I'm too young now."

Tía Magdalena thought for a while. When she answered, her voice was kind. "You can't simply

choose to be a curandera," she said. "You have to know
which herbs cure which ills, and you have to be obser-
vant and careful. But more than all that, you must be
a healer."

"A healer," repeated Josefina. "How will I know if
I'm a healer or not?"

"You'll know," said Tía Magdalena. "You'll know.
It will be clear to you and to everyone else if you are."

Josefina sighed. "I hope I am," she said.

"You'll find out," said Tía Magdalena. "In time."

While Tía Magdalena cleared up after their tea,
Josefina went back to the storeroom to finish dust-
ing. All the while, she was remembering what Tía
Magdalena had said. How she wished there were some
way to prove to Tía Magdalena that she was the right
kind of person to be a curandera!

Josefina looked at the big blue-and-white jar on
the shelf and thought about how it had been handed
down from curandera to curandera. The jar was dusty.
Surely Tía Magdalena would be pleased if she dusted
it as a surprise for her. Josefina stood on her tiptoes to
take the jar off the shelf. She could reach it with only
one hand. She tapped the jar to move it to the edge of

the shelf so that she could lift it off with both hands and . . . CRASH!

The jar fell to the floor and smashed into a thousand pieces. Josefina's heart stopped beating. For a terrible moment she stood still, staring in horror at what she had done. Then, without thinking, Josefina ran from the room. She flew past Tía Magdalena, out the door, and ran away as fast as she could.

Shame, shame, shame! The word pounded in Josefina's head with every step she took. Josefina ran without thinking about where she was going. Faster and faster she ran, out of the village, up the road to the rancho, toward the house, until she came to the orchard. She climbed up into her favorite apricot tree. Its branches were thickening with buds, but there were no blossoms to hide Josefina. *How could I have been so clumsy?* she thought. *Tía Magdalena treasured the blue-and-white jar, and I destroyed it. Then I ran away! What a stupid, childish thing to do! Not like a girl who's nearly ten. I'll never be able to face Tía Magdalena again!*

Josefina clung to the trunk, and hot tears ran down her cheeks. She had been sitting that way a while when she heard someone say, "Josefina?"

Josefina looked down through the branches and
saw Tía Dolores's face lifted toward her. Josefina felt
as if all her bones had melted. She slid down from
the tree right into Tía Dolores's arms and buried her
face in Tía Dolores's shoulder. Then she cried and
cried. Tía Dolores rubbed her back and let her cry.
When at last her sobs stopped, Tía Dolores put a
cool hand on Josefina's cheek and looked at her with
sympathetic eyes.

"Your papá went to Tía Magdalena's house to walk
home with you," said Tía Dolores. "She told him what
happened, and he told me."

"Is Tía Magdalena angry?" asked Josefina. "And
Papá, too?"

Tía Dolores smoothed Josefina's hair and said,
"They're sad and . . ."

"And disappointed," Josefina finished for her.
Roughly, Josefina wiped the tears off her cheeks. "I
broke Tía Magdalena's most precious jar. Then I made
it worse by running away. I ruined everything."

"Everything?" asked Tía Dolores.

Josefina was so ashamed and miserable she could
hardly speak. "I was hoping Tía Magdalena would

teach me to be a curandera when I am old enough,"
Josefina said. "Now she won't want to."

"Ah, I see," said Tía Dolores. "Can you tell me why
you want to be a curandera?"

"It's hard to explain," said Josefina. She put her
hand on her pouch and felt the root Tía Magdalena
had given her. "I like helping people feel better. And
I've . . . I've always wondered if there's a reason why
Mamá chose Tía Magdalena to be my godmother.
Maybe Mamá hoped I'd be a curandera."

"You mean, maybe she had the same hope for
you that you have for yourself," said Tía Dolores. She
hugged Josefina and said, "You know what you must
do right now, don't you?"

"Sí," said Josefina. "Sweep up the mess I made,
and apologize to Tía Magdalena."

"And you must ask her to give you a second
chance," said Tía Dolores.

Josefina sighed hopelessly.

Tía Dolores bent down so that her eyes were
level with Josefina's. "Spring is the season for second
chances," she said. "Didn't your mamá's flowers sprout
again? Didn't Sombrita get another chance to live when

you promised to take care of her?" Tía Dolores smiled. "We're all given second chances. We just have to be brave enough to take them."

Josefina hugged Tía Dolores. She hoped Tía Dolores was right. Oh, if Tía Magdalena would give her a second chance, she would be so grateful!

Tía Magdalena had only one thing to say after Josefina apologized. "The jar cannot be repaired," she said. "But perhaps your hopes can."

Whenever Josefina made up her mind to do something, it cheered her. She felt awful about what she had done at Tía Magdalena's. But she wasn't going to let her mistake kill her hopes. She still wanted to be a healer. Tía Magdalena had said that it would be clear to her and to everyone else if she was. She was determined to find out. Josefina kept the root Tía Magdalena had given her in her pouch as a reminder to herself.

It was cold and rainy. It seemed as if winter had returned. But finally, just the day before Josefina's birthday, the clouds brightened from gray to white and the sun shone. On that spring morning full of promise, Josefina set out with Papá and his servant Miguel to go to the pueblo.

Papá and Miguel were leading mules that were loaded down with blankets. The mules kicked up a lot of mud, so the blankets were wrapped in cloths to protect them. The path to the pueblo wound its way next to the stream. The banks were dotted with wild-flowers. In the trees above, birds sang loudly, trying to outdo one another. Josefina couldn't help feeling proud when she looked at the blankets. She had made some of them, and now Papá was going to trade them to his friend Esteban.

Josefina had another reason to be happy. She was going to see *her* friend Mariana, Esteban's grand-daughter. Josefina had tucked her doll, Niña, into her sash because Mariana liked to play dolls. And of course she'd brought along her faithful little shadow, Sombrita, to meet Mariana.

The pueblo was five long miles downstream from the rancho, and after the first mile Sombrita lagged. Josefina had to pick her up and carry her. Josefina was relieved when the stream widened and the pueblo seemed to appear all of a sudden. It rose up between the stream and the mountains. The pueblo was made of adobe just as Josefina's house was. But it was much taller than Josefina's house because several stories were built one on top of the other. Ladders led from level to level.

When Papá, Josefina, and Miguel arrived at the pueblo, they entered its big, clean-swept center plaza. There they were greeted by small children and curious dogs. Sombrita was timid. She hid her face in the crook of Josefina's elbow.

Esteban met them at his doorway. "Welcome," he said to Papá.

"Gracias, my friend," answered Papá. "May God bless you."

Miguel began to unload the blankets from the mules. Sombrita stayed with Miguel as Esteban led Papá and Josefina inside. They sat down by the fire, and almost immediately Mariana and her grandmother appeared with bowls of food. There were little pies with fruit inside and cups of hot tea. Mariana didn't say anything, but she smiled shyly at Josefina and her eyes had a welcome in them. Josefina smiled back. Both girls knew they shouldn't speak unless one of the grown-ups asked them a question. It wouldn't be good manners.

As they ate, Papá and Esteban talked about the weather, their crops, and their animals. Papá told Esteban about the meeting the village men had held to hear how much water each one would be allowed to use from the acequias. Esteban told Papá how much wool the spring sheepshearing had brought. Even though both men knew Papá had come to trade, they didn't talk about it. To begin by talking about business would be rude. Sometimes the two men just sat together in a comfortable silence. They seemed to have all the time in the world.

But Josefina was impatient. She couldn't wait to show Sombrita to Mariana. Josefina tried to sit as still as her friend did but it was hard. At last Papá and Esteban finished their food. As Mariana and her grandmother removed their bowls, Josefina admired the way Mariana moved so gracefully in her soft deerskin moccasins. Mariana wore a beautiful blanket draped over one shoulder and belted with a woven sash. Her bangs fell to her eyebrows, and her dark hair framed her face.

"My friend," said Esteban. "Thank you for bringing the blankets."

"Thank you for accepting them," said Papá. "I've brought sixty."

"Good," said Esteban. "When the sheep are old enough, I'll drive them to your rancho."

Papá nodded. This was the way he and Esteban had always traded. Nothing was written. Esteban's spoken promise was enough. Papá said that his family and Esteban's family had always respected each other and traded with each other fairly.

Josefina knew that this summer both Papá and Esteban were going to trade for the first time with the *americanos* who came to Santa Fe from the United States. Papá planned to trade mules, and Esteban would trade the blankets that Josefina and Papá had brought to him today.

"I hope trading with the americanos will be a good thing," Papá said.

Esteban nodded to show that he shared Papá's hope.

Then Mariana caught her grandfather's eye and

he smiled. Both Josefina and Mariana knew that was a sign that they could go. They stood up eagerly and hurried outside into the sunshine. Josefina picked up Sombrita and held her to face Mariana. "This is my Sombrita," she said. "We call her that because she follows me like a shadow wherever I go."

"Oh!" sighed Mariana. Her eyes were wide with delight. She scratched Sombrita behind her ear, just where the little goat liked it best. "Will Sombrita follow us to the stream?" Mariana asked.

"Of course!" said Josefina. "Watch!"

As Josefina and Mariana walked toward the stream, they peeked over their shoulders from time to time and shared a giggle at the sight of Sombrita following right on their heels. When they reached the stream, the girls found a sunny spot to play. Sombrita curled up in the warm grass and went to sleep. Josefina took her doll, Niña, out of her sash. Mariana had a doll too, made out of cornhusks. The girls pretended that their dolls were sisters. They made necklaces for them out of tiny wild-flowers, and boats from curves of bark.

They had just launched their boats in the stream when suddenly Josefina stood up. "Where is

Sombrita?" she asked Mariana. "I don't see her."

Mariana stood up, too. The girls shaded their eyes and looked all around. But the little black-and-white goat was nowhere to be seen. "We'll have to look for her," said Josefina. "She can't have gone very far." She tucked Niña into her sash and Mariana picked up her doll, and they walked along the narrow footpath that led downstream. Josefina hoped they were going in the right direction. She could still see the pueblo behind them, but it seemed to shrink smaller with every step they took. Both girls knew they should not be so far from the pueblo, but they *had* to find little Sombrita. They couldn't stop. The farther they went, the faster they walked, and the more worried they both became.

Neither girl said anything for a long while. Then Josefina spoke as if she were thinking aloud. "Sombrita's not lost," she said, trying not to sound shaky. "She's not lost until we stop trying to find her."

With anxious steps, the girls kept going. Just after they'd rounded the next bend in the path, Josefina squinted. She thought she saw something black and white in the grass ahead. Could it be? It was! Josefina's heart lifted. "Oh, Sombrita," she cried as she ran forward.

Sombrita didn't look at her. The goat was staring at something else with friendly curiosity, as if it might be a delightful new plaything.

When Josefina saw what it was, she stopped short. All her relief turned to horror. Between her and the little goat was a huge rattlesnake.

Josefina swallowed hard. She felt sweat on her forehead and an odd trembling in her stomach. The snake was coiled and ready to strike. Josefina heard its eerie rattle. She saw its scary, skinny tongue darting in and out of its mouth. She saw the snake's beady black eyes in their sunken sockets. Josefina bit her lip. The snake's cruel stare was fixed on Sombrita.

Rattlesnake

CHAPTER 4

Josefina," said Mariana in a low voice. She saw the snake, too.

Josefina signaled Mariana to stay back. She had only one thought. *She had to save Sombrita!* Ever so slowly, Josefina sank down and picked up a rock. She held it out behind her to Mariana. Mariana understood and silently stretched out her hand to take it.

When their hands touched, Josefina whispered, "I'm going to get Sombrita. Don't throw the rock unless the snake moves, because if you miss . . ."

Mariana squeezed Josefina's hand, then she took the rock.

Very, very slowly, Josefina edged forward. She made a wide arc around the snake. Inch by anxious inch she moved next to Sombrita who, for once, stood still. Josefina stooped, gathered Sombrita in her arms, and straightened. Then everything happened so fast it was a blur. The snake gave a menacing rattle. Mariana threw the rock at it and missed. The snake whipped its head around, shot forward, and struck Mariana on the arm with its fangs.

"Mariana!" cried Josefina as she saw her friend grab her arm and stumble back. Suddenly furious, Josefina put Sombrita down and snatched up a rock. She threw with all her might. The rock hit the snake in its middle. With one last sickening hiss, the snake slithered away so fast it seemed to simply disappear.

Mariana moaned, sinking to her knees as if all the strength had gone out of her. She didn't cry, but her breath was ragged. Her eyes were shut tight.

Josefina bent over her friend. "Let me see your arm," she said. Gently, Josefina took Mariana's arm in her hands. She couldn't help gasping when she saw two tiny holes where the snake's fangs had sunk in. The wound was an ugly purplish color, and it was already beginning to swell. In her mind, Josefina heard Tía Magdalena's voice saying, *If you don't get the venom out right away, it can kill you.* Josefina spoke with urgency to Mariana. "We've got to get back to the pueblo," she said. "We need help."

Mariana tried to stand but dropped back on her knees. "I can't . . . I can't go that far," she said in a hoarse whisper.

Josefina's heart twisted with fear. She knelt down and something hard in her pouch thunked against her. It was the globe mallow root Tía Magdalena had given her. Without hesitating, Josefina took it out. She crushed the root between two rocks and spit on it to make it pasty. Then she pressed it against Mariana's arm where the snake had struck. She squeezed Mariana's arm gently to bring the venom up. Mariana whimpered, but she didn't pull her arm away.

Again and again, Josefina pressed the crushed root against the wound. Again and again, she pressed Mariana's arm. Again and again and again . . . Josefina knew she had to stay calm, but she had to fight against a rising feeling of panic. The globe mallow didn't seem to be working! Mariana's arm was still swollen and bruised-looking. Oh, how long would it take? What if she was using the root the wrong way? Perhaps she had misunderstood. What would happen to Mariana if the venom poisoned her blood? If only someone would come to help!

But no one came. The minutes felt like hours. Josefina was just about to give up and run for help when—oh, at last!—she heard Mariana take a deep, shuddery breath. Mariana opened her eyes, and color came back to her face.

Josefina said a quick, silent prayer of thanks. Then she asked Mariana, "Do you think you can walk if I help you?"

Mariana nodded.

Carefully, Josefina helped Mariana stand. Mariana looped her good arm over Josefina's shoulder, and Josefina put her own arm behind Mariana's back to support her. "Lean on me," Josefina said. Then she turned and looked down at Sombrita. "Listen," she said to the little goat. "Now you must really be my *sombrita,* my little shadow. Stay right behind me. Do you understand?"

Sombrita seemed to. She stayed close to Josefina and Mariana every step of the weary walk back. Slowly, the two girls trudged along the path next to the stream. Slowly, they trudged up the long incline to the pueblo. Josefina knew they had been gone a long time, and Papá and Esteban would be worried. But she and Mariana could not move fast. Their tired feet dragged. Their tired shoulders drooped. They were only halfway between the stream and the pueblo when Josefina saw Papá and Esteban coming toward them. She had never been so glad to see anyone in her life!

Papá and Esteban rushed to the girls, and Josefina saw that their faces were tight with worry. Mariana said quickly, "A rattlesnake bit me, but Josefina knew what to do." She smiled weakly at Josefina. "Tell them," she said.

Papá and Esteban stared at Josefina, but she was too worn out to explain. Instead she held out her hand to show them the crushed root. "It draws the venom out," she said. "I had it in my pouch."

Esteban's expression did not change. His voice was very deep when he said, "Gracias, Josefina. Gracias." He lifted Mariana up. Papá, Josefina, and Sombrita followed them the rest of the way back to the pueblo.

Later, as they were walking home to the rancho,
Papá asked Josefina to tell him the whole story of
what had happened. So Josefina did. She didn't leave
out anything, even though she was out of breath
because she had to take two steps for every one of
Papá's. They hadn't gone very far before Papá lifted
both Josefina and Sombrita up onto a mule's back.
After that Josefina couldn't see Papá's face, but somehow she knew that he was still listening hard to every
word she said.

Josefina opened one sleepy eye. Could she be
dreaming? It was not quite dawn, and yet she seemed
to hear music. She sat up. Her sisters Francisca and
Clara were gone from the room that they shared with
her. Suddenly, Josefina grinned to herself. She remembered what day it was: the feast day of San José and
her birthday.

Very slowly, the door to her room opened. In the
pearly morning light she saw Papá, Tía Dolores, Ana
and her husband Tomás, Francisca, Clara, Carmen the
cook, and her husband Miguel. They began to sing:

On the day you were born
All the beautiful flowers were born,
The sun and moon were born,
And all the stars.

In the middle of the song, Sombrita poked her head around the corner of the door and bleated as if she were singing, too. Everyone laughed, and Tía Dolores said, "We wanted to surprise you with a lovely morning song, but I think someone forgot the words!"

Josefina picked up Sombrita and gave her a hug. "Gracias," she said to everyone, feeling a little shy at all the attention. "I liked it."

The morning song was only the first surprise in a day full of them. Ana made cookies called *bizcochitos* for everyone to eat before breakfast. At morning prayers, Francisca showed Josefina how she'd decorated the family altar with garlands of mint and willow leaves and how she'd surrounded the statue of San José, the saint Josefina was named for, with white wild lilies and little yellow celery flowers. Clara, who liked to be practical, surprised Josefina by helping with her chores.

But when it was time to dress for the party, Clara
had an impractical surprise for Josefina. It was a
dainty pair of turquoise blue slippers. "It's about time
I handed these down to you," said Clara. "I hardly
ever wear them."

"Oh, Clara!" said Josefina, very pleased. She put
the slippers on. They were only a *little* too big for her.

"If you're going to be so elegant," said Francisca,
"you'd better carry Mamá's fan."

"And wear Mamá's shawl!" said Ana.

The four sisters shared Mamá's fan and shawl
and brought them out only on very special occasions.
Josefina swirled the shawl around her shoulders and
looked behind her to see the brilliant embroidered
flowers and the slippery, shimmery fringe on the back.
She fluttered the fan and felt very elegant indeed.

The party table looked elegant, too. There was a
beautiful cloth on it, and the family's best plates and
glasses and silverware. Tía Dolores had made a special
fancy loaf of bread. There were meat turnovers, and
fruit tarts, and candied fruit that looked like jewels.
But best of all, in the center of the table there was a
red jar with one small branch of apricot blossoms in

it. Josefina smiled when she saw the perfect blossoms. She knew that Tía Dolores had cut the branch from *her* tree—the tree she liked to climb. Josefina remembered the day Tía Dolores had comforted her next to that apricot tree. "We're all given second chances," Tía Dolores had said. "We just have to be brave enough to take them."

Soon music and laughter and happy voices swirled around the beautiful table. Friends and neighbors and workers from the rancho arrived bringing small gifts of dried fruit or nuts, sweets, or chocolate for Josefina. Esteban and Mariana brought a wonderful gift. It was a melon that had been buried in sand since last fall's harvest to keep it fresh.

When Josefina thanked her, Mariana said, "It's not much, but my heart goes with it."

Papá quieted everyone. "Today is the feast of San José," he said, "and today my daughter Josefina is ten years old. I'm going to tell you a story about her." Josefina felt Mariana's hand slip into her own. They both stood still, eyes shyly cast down, while Papá told the story of the rattlesnake. Papá began at the beginning and told everything that had happened. He described

the snake in such a scary way it made everyone shiver.
When the story was finished, Papá called Josefina to
him. He handed her something that looked sort of like a
shell. It was rattles from a rattlesnake. "I've saved these
since I was a boy just your age," said Papá to Josefina,
"to remind me of something I was proud of. Now I am
giving them to you, because I am proud of you."

Everyone clapped, and Papá leaned down to kiss
Josefina's cheek. Josefina thought she had never in her
life felt so happy or so proud.

Suddenly, Tía Magdalena was by her side. "Dear
child," she said.

Josefina smiled. She held out her hand to show
Tía Magdalena the snake's rattles. "I'm going to put
these in my memory box," she said. "They'll remind me
of the moment when I found out something important
about myself. I found out that I am a healer."

Tía Magdalena smiled deep into Josefina's eyes.
"Sí," she said simply. "You are."

Later that evening, when the party was over,
Josefina and Papá walked to the goats' pen together.

They wanted to check on Sombrita, who had not been invited to the party. Sombrita was fast asleep.

"It's unusual to see her so still, isn't it?" said Josefina. She and Papá smiled, looking at the peaceful goat.

"She's healthy and lively," said Papá. "She might not have been, if you hadn't kept your promise to take care of her after Florecita died. You gave her a second chance at life."

Papá and Josefina walked back to the house. On the hillside, the flowering fruit trees in the orchard were lit by the moon, as if a pale cloud had settled on them. The night air was cool, but softened by the scent of blossoms. Josefina took a deep breath. She thought the air smelled like apricots.

"Papá," she said. "We're all given second chances. We just have to be brave enough to take them. That's what Tía Dolores says."

"Does she?" asked Papá. "Does she indeed?"

The Bird-Shaped Flute

igh up on a breezy hilltop, Josefina sat playing her clay flute. The flute was shaped like a bird and sounded like one, too. When Josefina played it, a clear, fine tune just like a bird's whistle looped through the air into the blue, blue sky.

The soft days of spring had flown by swiftly, and now it was July. Josefina and her family were visiting her grandfather's rancho, which was about a mile from the center of Santa Fe. Josefina loved this hilltop behind Abuelito's house. From here she could see the flat rooftops of buildings in Santa Fe and the narrow streets that zigzagged between them. She could see the slender silvery ribbon that was the Santa Fe River, and the long road that led home to Papá's rancho fifteen miles away.

A few days ago, Josefina, her papá, two of her

sisters, and Tía Dolores, had traveled on that road to come to Abuelito's rancho. The trip was hot and dusty, but Josefina had been too excited to mind. She and her family had worked, planned, and looked forward to the trip for almost a year.

They were traveling for a very important reason. They needed to be in Santa Fe when the wagon train from the United States arrived. Papá had brought mules and blankets with him to trade with the americanos. Josefina understood how much depended on this trade. If the americanos paid well for the mules and the blankets, Papá would be able to replace his sheep that had been killed in a terrible flood last fall. If Papá could not replace the sheep, it would be a hard, hungry winter for everyone on the rancho. They needed sheep for food and for wool to weave. Josefina had prayed and prayed that Papá's trading with the americanos would go well.

Josefina and her sisters couldn't wait to see the fine and fancy things the americanos would bring. There'd be toys and shoes and material for dresses that had come hundreds of miles on the Santa Fe Trail, all the way from the United States! The wagon train was expected to arrive any day now, and Josefina was keeping a lookout for it. As soon as she'd finished her chores this morning, she'd climbed up here to her favorite hilltop to look at the southeast horizon. She was hoping to see a cloud of dust stirred up by the wagon train, but the horizon looked the same as always.

Just now, though, Josefina *heard* something new. It sounded as if a real bird were singing along with her clay flute. Josefina stopped playing and tilted her head to listen. Then she grinned. It wasn't a real bird at all. It was a person whistling.

"Buenos días!" Josefina called out. She turned, expecting to see that the whistler was one of her sisters who'd come to watch for the wagon train, too. But it wasn't. The whistler was a young man Josefina had never seen before. Josefina scrambled to her feet so quickly she almost dropped her flute. The young man was a stranger. And not just any stranger, either. Josefina immediately folded her hands, bowed her head, and looked down at the ground, which was the polite way for a child to stand before an adult. But she could tell just by looking at the tips of the stranger's boots that they came from the United States. She knew because Abuelito had a pair of boots like them that he'd bought last summer from the americanos.

"Buenos días," said the young man. He spoke in Spanish, but with an accent Josefina had never heard before.

Josefina had a sudden, excited thought. The young man must be an americano who'd come ahead of the wagon train! Josefina was usually shy around strangers, but right now her curiosity was stronger than her shyness. If the young man was an americano, he'd be the first she'd ever met face to face. She raised her eyes and sneaked a peek. He had a very *nice* face, Josefina decided. He had blue eyes, a sunburned nose, and a friendly smile.

"Forgive me for surprising you," the stranger went on. "I thought you were a bird."

I thought you were a bird, too! Josefina almost said. She wanted to ask, *Please, señor, who* are *you?* But of course she didn't. It wasn't good manners for a child to ask a grown-up questions. In fact, Josefina wasn't sure whether it was proper for her to talk to the stranger at all. Perhaps she should *act* like a bird and fly away! But that didn't seem very polite.

While Josefina stood wondering what she should do, the young man did something astonishing. He took a case off his back, opened it, took out a violin, and began to play. Josefina smiled when she realized that he was playing the same notes that she had played on her bird-shaped flute. The young man wound the notes together into a tune that danced in the air. When he finished, he swept his hat off his head and bowed. "I'm Patrick O'Toole, from Missouri," he said. "What is your name?"

"By God's grace," Josefina answered, "I am Josefina Montoya."

"Josefina Montoya," Patrick repeated slowly. "I'm glad to meet you. I'm looking for the home of Señor Felipe Romero. Do you know him?"

"Sí," answered Josefina politely. "He's my grand-father." She pointed to Abuelito's house nearby. "He lives right there."

"Well, then, Señorita Josefina," said Patrick as he put his violin away. "Will you lead me to your grand-father's house?"

"I will," answered Josefina. "Please, follow me." She slipped the string of her clay flute around her neck and led Patrick down the hill. She couldn't help smiling a secret smile when she thought how surprised her family would be!

Abuelito's house was built around a center courtyard. The doors to the kitchen, the sleeping rooms, the weaving room, and the family sala opened onto it. Josefina led Patrick across the courtyard. She stopped outside the family sala, where her family was gathering for the mid-day meal. Abuelito had come to the door and was staring out at her.

"Abuelito," Josefina said respectfully. "Please permit me to introduce Señor Patrick O'Toole, from"—Josefina pronounced the English word carefully— "Missouri."

Abuelito was used to having unexpected guests, but this was the first time one of his granddaughters had brought a complete stranger to visit. And the stranger was an americano, too! But Abuelito was always a gracious host. "*Bienvenido,*" he said to Patrick. "You are welcome in my house, young man. Please come in."

"Thank you, sir," said Patrick. Josefina tapped her head to warn him to duck down so that he'd fit under the low doorway, and they both stepped inside. "I know you were expecting my father, who did business with you last summer, but—"

"Oh!" said Abuelito as he realized who Patrick was. "You're the son of my friend, Señor O'Toole." Abuelito shook Patrick's hand. "Your father is a fine man. I hope he's in good health?"

"I believe so," said Patrick. "You see, he's farther south in Mexico, so he asked me to conduct his business here in—"

"Fine, fine," interrupted Abuelito. "There will be time for us to talk about business later, plenty of time."

Josefina could see that Patrick didn't understand. Abuelito would consider it very poor manners to discuss business matters right away, especially with someone he did not know. It was the custom in New Mexico to have a friendly conversation first, *then* talk about business.

Patrick tried again. "Well, sir," he began. No one saw Josefina tug on his sleeve. When Patrick glanced at her, she frowned and shook her head just the smallest bit to tell him no. Patrick looked confused for a moment, but then he seemed to understand. "As you say, sir," he said to Abuelito. "We can talk about business later."

"Good!" said Abuelito. "Allow me to introduce you to my family." He introduced Patrick to Papá, and then to Abuelita, Josefina's grandmother, and then to Tía Dolores.

"We're so glad Dolores is home for a visit," Abuelito said. "She's been away, staying on my son-in-law's rancho for almost a year now, helping him take care of his daughters since his own dear wife died. You've already met his youngest daughter, Josefina. His eldest, Ana, stayed home to help her husband look after the rancho. These are his daughters Francisca and Clara."

The sisters stood with their heads bowed. But Josefina saw Francisca studying Patrick from under her long, dark eyelashes.

"Please sit and have something to eat, señor," said Abuelita generously. "Honor us by joining us."

"Gracias," said Patrick.

Josefina sat between Francisca and Clara. Both sisters poked her and looked at her with raised eyebrows that said silently in sister language, *Oh, we can't wait to find out how you met the americano!* Josefina grinned back, pleased to have made her sisters curious.

During the meal, Abuelito kept the conversation away from business. He spoke to Patrick about the beautiful summer weather they were having and asked

Patrick about weather in Missouri. Abuelita said nothing, but her sharp eyes never left Patrick's face. Papá didn't say anything either. But Josefina could tell that he was listening carefully to everything Patrick said.

I hope Papá likes Señor Patrick, Josefina thought. *I hope everyone does.* She was glad when Tía Dolores said to Patrick, "You speak Spanish well. How did you learn?"

"My father taught me," said Patrick. "I can't read or write Spanish at all, and I'm afraid I don't always remember the right words to say."

"You are doing fine," said Abuelito kindly.

In fact, Josefina thought Patrick was doing beautifully. He stumbled over his words only once, and that was when Francisca poured him some tea. Patrick looked up at her and seemed to forget how to say thank you—or anything else. But Josefina had seen *that* happen to men who spoke perfect Spanish. Francisca was very beautiful.

Finally everyone had finished eating and the servants had cleared the table. Abuelito turned to Patrick. "Now," he said. "Tell us. When will the wagon train arrive?"

"Tomorrow morning, sir," said Patrick.

"That's good news!" said Abuelito. "But how is it that you are here before the rest of the wagon train?"

"I'm one of the scouts," explained Patrick. "Scouts ride ahead of the wagon train. We find the safest places to cross rivers, the easiest passes through the mountains, and the best places to set up camp along the way."

"I'm sure you've had lots of adventures," said Abuelito.

"Not as many as you have, sir," said Patrick. "My father told me that you've been a trader on the *Camino Real* for many years. He said you've had adventures enough for twenty men!"

Abuelito was pleased. "I'll tell you about my adventures on the Camino Real sometime," he said.

"I'd like that," said Patrick. "You see, I'll be here in Santa Fe for about a week. I have to be ready to leave at a moment's notice. As soon as the captain of the wagon train gives me the word, I'll be heading down the Camino Real. Many of the americano traders are continuing farther south into Mexico when they leave Santa Fe, so the scouts have to go ahead of them and explore the route. Anything you can tell me would be a great help, Señor Romero."

"It will be a pleasure," said Abuelito.

"Thank you, sir," said Patrick. "Maybe you can help me in another way, too. The traders are going to need fresh mules for their trip down the Camino Real. They asked me to find some. Do you know anyone who has mules to sell or trade?"

Abuelito didn't answer right away. He glanced at Papá.

Josefina knew that Abuelito and Papá were being careful. Before they decided to do business with Patrick, they'd want to be sure he was honest and trustworthy. Papá had been watching Patrick as if he were trying to decide what sort of person the young man was.

Now Papá spoke slowly. "I have mules to trade," he said.

"Oh!" said Patrick. "May I see them, Señor Montoya?"

Papá nodded. "You may see them," he said. "Come with me." He stood and gestured toward the door.

Abuelito went outside and Patrick started to follow. But before he left, Patrick thanked Abuelita for her hospitality. Then he turned and smiled at Josefina. "I certainly am glad I heard that bird whistling on the hilltop," he said. "I hope I'll hear it again soon!"

Josefina smiled back.

After the men had left, Josefina and her sisters helped Abuelita and Tía Dolores tidy the room.

"So!" said Francisca to Josefina. "Where did you find the americano?"

"Well, I guess he found me," said Josefina. "I was on the hilltop looking for the wagon train and he surprised me."

"And *you* surprised *me,* Josefina," said Tía Dolores. She put her hands on her hips and smiled at Josefina. "I've always believed that you were shy of strangers. Not anymore, I see!"

"You and the americano seem to have become acquainted very quickly," said Clara.

"Too quickly," said Abuelita, frowning. "We don't really know this americano at all. How do we know he is truly Señor O'Toole's son? How do we know he is honest?" She shook her head. "All we know for certain is that he's very young. I hope your papá will be careful. I don't think it's wise to trust a stranger, especially when the business is so important!"

"Nothing is decided yet," said Tía Dolores quietly.

Abuelita went on. "If this young man isn't reliable, it'll be a terrible mistake to do business with him," she said.

Abuelita sighed and Josefina's shoulders drooped. She had been so proud to be the one who brought Patrick to her family! Would Papá be wrong to trust Patrick? Was *she* wrong to like Patrick?

Tía Dolores moved closer to Josefina. "How *did* you get acquainted with Señor Patrick so quickly?" she asked.

Josefina held up the little bird-shaped flute. "I was playing this clay flute that you gave me," she said. "Then Señor Patrick played the same song on his violin." She smiled, remembering. "The music sounded so friendly."

Tía Dolores laughed. "Music *can* sound friendly," she said. "Sometimes music can say things better than words can. Don't you think so, Josefina?"

"Sí!" said Josefina, cheered by Tía Dolores's understanding. She hurried to finish helping so that she could go outside. She wanted to play Patrick's song on her bird-shaped flute.

Heart's Desire

 his is a day I'll remember as long as I live, thought Josefina. She was holding Tía Dolores's hand, and she gave it a squeeze. Tía Dolores smiled down at Josefina's glowing, upturned face. "Any minute now," Tía Dolores said. They were standing in a crowd that had gathered in front of the Palace of the Governors in Santa Fe. Everyone was waiting, waiting, *waiting* for the wagon train to pull into town. *Any minute now,* thought Josefina with a delighted shiver. *Any minute!*

Soon after dawn while the air was still cool, Josefina and her family and one of Abuelita's servants had walked into Santa Fe. Abuelita had stayed home because she didn't like crowds. But everyone else was eager to join the people gathering to see the wagon train. All along the road, they saw tents that had sprung up overnight. Indians had come with pottery and blankets and horses to trade. Fur trappers had come down from the mountains. Soldiers had come from their fort up on the hill. People had come from villages and ranchos for miles around. They all gathered in the plaza that was in the center of Santa Fe. Even the long, low adobe buildings built around all four sides of the plaza seemed to lean forward expectantly, looking for the wagon train.

Josefina had never seen so many people! Words in different languages swirled around her in a confused jumble, until suddenly she heard one shout above the others.

"The wagons! The americanos! The wagon train is here!" someone called out. Then many voices rose up together in a roar. Church bells rang. Josefina's heart was pounding. She called out with the others, "The wagon train is here!"

Around Josefina, many people were clapping, cheering, and waving as the americanos' wagons lumbered into view. But other people were not so enthusiastic. They stood quietly, arms crossed over their chests, watching the wagons with questioning looks, as if they were not convinced that the arrival of the americanos was a good thing. Josefina stood on tiptoe to see the wagons better. But she didn't let go of Tía Dolores's hand, and she was glad to be safely wedged between Tía Dolores and Papá. The wagons were so heavy they rumbled like the thunder of an oncoming storm and made the earth shake under Josefina's feet.

The americanos driving the wagons whooped and hooted and whistled and threw their hats into the air. They circled their whips and then snapped them so that they made a *pop!* as loud as a gunshot. Wagon after wagon rolled into the plaza. Josefina counted more than twenty. Some were pulled by plodding oxen that seemed half asleep in spite of all the noise. But most of the wagons were pulled by mules that pricked up their ears and looked pleased at all the attention.

"Tía Dolores," said Josefina. "Look how big the wagons are!"

The wagons *were* enormous. Their wheels stood higher than Josefina's head! Some of the wagons were flying a flag different from the Mexican flag Josefina was used to. This flag was red, white, and blue. The flag's stripes and stars looked snappy and clean in the bright sunshine. Josefina thought the americanos looked cleaned up, too, as if that morning they'd scrubbed their faces, slicked down their hair, put on their Sunday-best clothes, and polished the dust of hundreds of miles off their boots. Some of the men looked rough, while others looked quiet and well mannered. But to Josefina's eyes, *all* the americanos looked glad to be in Santa Fe and at the end of the trail at last.

Papá bent his head toward Tía Dolores so she could hear him above the hubbub. "Your father and I are going to look for Señor Patrick at the customs house," he said. "The americanos have to go there to make a list of their goods and to pay taxes. The servant will stay with you and the girls."

Tía Dolores nodded. "Very well," she said. "Go ahead."

But Papá didn't go. His eyes had a twinkle in them as he looked at Tía Dolores. "Have you told the girls?" he asked her.

"Not yet," answered Tía Dolores.

"Told us what?" asked Francisca immediately.

Papá laughed. "Tell them," he said to Tía Dolores. "After all, it was your idea. We wouldn't have as much to trade today if it were not for you." His voice was full of gratitude and affection. Tía Dolores smiled, and then Papá went off with Abuelito to find Patrick.

"Please, Tía Dolores! Tell us what Papá meant!" begged the sisters.

Tía Dolores's eyes were shining. "Your papá and I think that you girls deserve something for all the hard work you've done weaving," she said. "We've decided that you may each choose one of the blankets you wove, and you may sell it or trade it for anything you wish."

"*Oh!*" gasped Francisca and Clara. "How wonderful!"

Josefina didn't say anything. Instead, she hugged Tía Dolores. Josefina and her sisters had never expected to use the blankets they'd woven to get anything for themselves. *It's just like Tía Dolores to think of something so generous,* thought Josefina.

"Well!" said Francisca. She had an eager gleam in her eyes. "We'd better look around and decide what we'll get with our blankets."

There was certainly much to see! Tía Dolores and the sisters walked slowly around the plaza to watch the americanos unload their wagons. Some of the americanos had rented small stores to display their wares. Others had wooden stalls or spaces on the street where they set out their goods. Never in her life had Josefina imagined such a variety of things. She saw bolts of brightly colored cottons, wools, and silks. There were veils, shawls, sashes, and ribbons. There were shoes and hats, boots and stockings, combs, brushes, toothbrushes, and even silver toothpicks!

Clara stood for a long time studying pots and pans until Francisca dragged her away to look at buttons and jewelry she saw sparkling ahead. Clara stopped halfway there to gaze at knitting needles. Tía Dolores was distracted by some books, and the girls were fascinated by the mirrors that reflected their delighted faces. Many people were crowded around the watches and clocks, and even more were crowded around the tools. A few people were paying for the americanos' goods with silver coins, but most people were trading or swapping. Josefina saw a man from the pueblo swap a beautiful pottery jar he'd made for an americano's glass bottle. A fur trapper traded a bear skin for a hunting knife.

There were so many things, Josefina didn't know how she'd ever choose something for herself. Then Tía Dolores and the girls stopped in front of a trader who had toys among his goods. One toy in particular caught Josefina's eye. It was a little toy farm carved out of wood.

"Oh, look!" said Josefina as she knelt in front of it. There was a tiny cow, a horse pulling a cart, a goat, and a funny pink pig standing in front of a white stable. Two green trees shaded a painted house with a white fence behind it.

"You can almost hear the cow moo, can't you?" someone joked. It was Patrick. He and Papá and Abuelito had finished their business and had come to find Tía Dolores and the girls. "That reminds me of how the farms look back home in Missouri."

Josefina imagined what it would be like to sit in the shade of the two green trees or climb on the white fence. "I wish I could magically shrink," she said to Patrick. "I'd like to go inside the house. I've never seen a house that's so straight up and down, with such a steep roof and so many big windows!"

"It's different, isn't it?" said Patrick. "Here in New Mexico your houses are low. They look like they grew right up out of the ground because they're made out of earth, and they don't have any sharp corners. Where I come from the buildings seem to want to stick up and call attention to themselves. Sort of like the people, I guess!"

"I think the farm is very pretty," said Josefina. "I like it."

Clara looked over Josefina's shoulder. "But it's just a toy, Josefina," she said. "You shouldn't waste your blanket on *that*!"

Josefina sighed. Clara was being sensible, as usual. But Josefina couldn't help wanting the farm. She was sure it would be fun to play with the pink pig! And knowing that the little farm reminded Patrick of his home made Josefina like it even more.

Papá looped his finger around one of Josefina's braids and moved the braid behind her ear. Then he stooped and spoke softly so that only Josefina could hear. "We'll come back," he said kindly. "And you can look at the toy farm again." Josefina looked into his understanding brown eyes. "If that's what you want, then that's what you should get," Papá said. "Don't let anyone talk you out of your heart's desire."

Papá took Josefina's hand and stood up straight. Then in a louder voice he said to Tía Dolores, "I have good news. Señor Patrick has found traders who want to buy all of our mules."

"Oh?" said Tía Dolores. Her eyes had a question in them.

"Sí," answered Papá. His voice was serious and sure. "I have decided to let Señor Patrick trade the mules for us. He knows the americano traders. He can speak English to them. And he has promised to get me a good price."

"My friends will be glad to get the mules," said Patrick quickly. "Mules are sturdy. They do better than oxen on the wagon trails. Oxen are fussy eaters. They have delicate feet, and they get sunburned." Patrick pointed to his own red nose and joked, "Just like me!" Everyone laughed, and Patrick went on. "I can get you silver for the mules," he said.

Silver! This was lucky indeed. Normally, Papá would have traded the mules for goods from the americanos. Then he would trade the goods for sheep. Josefina knew Papá must be pleased. It would be much easier to buy the sheep they needed with silver.

"Señor Montoya, may I come by later today to get the mules?" Patrick asked Papá. "I can bring some of your silver today, and the rest at the end of the week after I've sold all the mules."

"Very well," said Papá. "I know I can trust you to keep your word." He and Patrick shook hands to seal their agreement. Josefina saw that Papá's grasp was firm. *Oh, I am so glad Papá has decided to trust Señor Patrick,* thought Josefina.

Abuelito seemed glad, too. "When you come for the mules, you must stay for dinner," he said to Patrick. "We'll celebrate!"

"And please remember to bring your violin," said Tía Dolores. "We can't celebrate without music!"

"I'll remember," said Patrick. He said *adiós* to everyone. Then he strolled away, cheerfully whistling Josefina's bird song.

A Charm from the Sky

ater that afternoon, Patrick came to Abuelito's rancho to get Papá's mules. He was going to take them back to Santa Fe after dinner. Josefina had climbed to her hilltop to meet him and lead him to the house.

Before they started down the hill, Patrick tilted his head back and said, "I've never seen a sky so blue."

"Mamá used to say the sky is that blue because it's the bottom of heaven," said Josefina.

Patrick smiled. He pulled a small brass telescope out of his coat pocket. As Josefina watched, he focused the telescope on a point to the southeast. "Look through there," he said as he handed her the telescope.

Josefina focused the telescope for herself. "I see San Miguel Chapel," she said. She recognized the church easily even though it was far away. It came

clearly into view through the telescope, as if someone had painted a perfect picture of it in a tiny round
frame.

"Well," said Patrick, "yesterday I climbed up to the
bell of San Miguel Chapel. While I was up there a little
bit of the sky fell off, right into my hand. See?"

Josefina giggled when she looked. Patrick held a
small chunk of turquoise in his hand. The turquoise
was the same glorious blue as the sky.

Patrick tossed the chunk of turquoise up in the air,
caught it with the same hand, and put it in his pocket.
"Now I'll have a little bit of New Mexican sky with
me even when I go back home," he said, patting his
pocket as if he had a treasure in it. Then he pretended
to frown. "What's this?" he asked. He pulled a sheet
of paper out of the same pocket, unfolded it, and then
handed it to Josefina with a grin. "I believe this is for
you, Señorita Josefina."

"Gracias!" said Josefina. The paper was sheet
music. It had the notes and the words to a song printed
on it. Josefina couldn't read the words because they
were in English. She didn't know how to read the
notes, either, which were lined up like orderly black

birds on straight black branches. But she had seen sheet music before. Tía Dolores had some. "Perhaps when we go home, Tía Dolores will teach me to play this song on the piano," Josefina said to Patrick. "She knows how to read music. I think Papá does, too, unless he's forgotten." Josefina hesitated, then said, "Papá used to play the violin."

"Did he?" asked Patrick.

"Sí," said Josefina. She looked down at the sheet music and said quietly, "He used to play when Mamá was alive. But when . . . when she died, he gave his violin away. I think he was just too sad to play it anymore. We were all too sad for music for a long, long time." Josefina looked up at Patrick. "It's been better since Tía Dolores came to stay with us. We've all been happier, especially Papá. And Tía Dolores loves music. She even brought her piano with her when she came up the Camino Real from Mexico City with Abuelito's caravan. You should hear Abuelito tell *that* story!"

"He promised to tell me some of his adventures," said Patrick as they headed down the hill to the house. "If I ask, do you think he'll tell me the piano story this evening?"

"With pleasure!" answered Josefina. She knew there was nothing in the world Abuelito liked better than telling a story!

It was with *great* pleasure that Abuelito told the piano story and many other stories about the Camino Real during dinner. Then Patrick told stories about the Santa Fe Trail. He talked about herds of buffalo so endless they made the plains look black, and rivers so wide you could not see across them.

After dinner, Patrick took out his violin. He played such lively tunes that he soon had everyone clapping their hands and tapping their feet. The sun set and the fire was lit, but the moon poured so much silvery light into the room that they didn't need to light candles. Patrick's music was merry and lighthearted, full of fancy, funny twists and turns. Abuelito kept time slapping his leg, and Abuelita's dangling earrings swung and sparkled as she nodded her head to the rhythm of the music.

Patrick played and played. He was right in the middle of a song when, in one smooth movement, before anyone realized what he was doing, he handed his violin to Papá, saying, "Now it's your turn, Señor Montoya."

Suddenly, the room was completely quiet.

What is Señor Patrick doing? worried Josefina. *I told him Papá didn't play anymore!*

But Papá did not frown. Slowly, as if he were both eager and reluctant at the same time, Papá tucked Patrick's violin under his chin. He held the slender neck of the violin in his broad hand and delicately ran the bow over the strings. Chills ran up and down Josefina's spine.

"What shall I play?" Papá asked.

No one answered.

Josefina hopped up and put the sheet music Patrick had given her in front of Papá. "Play this, Papá," she said.

Papá began to play. He played softly at first, but every note became surer. Then Patrick began to sing the words. His voice was husky and low. Though Josefina could not understand the English words he was singing, she understood the wistful feeling of the song. Patrick sang:

'Mid pleasures and palaces though we may roam,
Be it ever so humble there's no place like home;
A charm from the skies seems to hallow us there,
Which seek through the world, is ne'er met with
elsewhere.

Patrick stopped singing. But Papá continued to play, making up a song that blended Patrick's song with an old Spanish song. Josefina sat still, listening intently, with her eyes fixed on Papá's face. Josefina knew that Papá's song was telling a story full of longing and hope.

Josefina wished the music would never end. Tía Dolores must have felt the same way. As the last note faded, she sighed a sigh that seemed to come straight from her heart. "Oh," she said to Papá. "That was lovely!"

Papá handed the violin back to Patrick, then smiled at Tía Dolores.

In that moment, Josefina knew what she wanted to trade for her blanket. She knew without a doubt what her heart's desire was.

She wanted Patrick's violin for Papá.

"No."

It was much later. Patrick had left, taking Papá's mules with him.

"No," said Clara again. She and Josefina and Francisca were in the sleeping sala they shared. All three were sitting on the bed Josefina and Clara slept in. But the sisters weren't even close to sleeping. They were having an argument. "I won't," said Clara flatly. "It's just not sensible."

Josefina and Francisca shared an exasperated look.

"But Clara," pleaded Francisca, who had agreed with Josefina's plan right away. "We need your blanket, too. It will work only if we all do it. Patrick's violin is worth at *least* three blankets."

"How about Ana's blanket?" asked Clara.

"We couldn't use it without asking her," said Josefina. "Anyway, Tía Dolores is going to trade it for boots for Ana's little boys."

"I want to trade my blanket for something practical, too!" said Clara. "It's different for you. You want that silly toy farm, and Francisca wants a mirror, which is just a luxury. I want useful things like knitting needles."

"Clara," coaxed Francisca. "When we go home, I will give you all of my knitting needles. I promise. They're good as new."

"Because you never use them!" said Clara. "Besides, I could get lots more than knitting needles. The americanos pay well for woven blankets."

Francisca started to say something sharp, but Josefina spoke first. "Didn't you see how happy Papá looked while he was playing Señor Patrick's violin?" Josefina asked Clara. "We have to get it for him. We just have to."

"Señor Patrick will probably say no anyway," said Clara stubbornly.

But Josefina could be stubborn, too. "We've got to at least *ask* him," she said. She looked straight into Clara's eyes and said something she *knew* would convince her to cooperate. "The truth is, it isn't only Papá's happiness I'm thinking of. You must have seen how much Tía Dolores loved it when Papá played. She's been so kind to us. Don't you think we owe it to her to please her if we can? Think how happy she would be at home if Papá played the violin while she played her piano."

Clara groaned and flopped facedown on the bed. But Josefina knew that by now she was only pretending to be cross. "Oh, all right!" Clara said, her voice muffled. "I'll do it! May God forgive me for being so foolish!"

Josefina and Francisca smiled at each other in triumph. They knew Clara couldn't refuse a chance to make Papá *and* Tía Dolores happy.

The next afternoon, the sun shone down straight and strong. It baked out the spicy scent of the *piñón* trees as the sisters and Tía Dolores walked to the plaza. A servant was with them because it wasn't safe while the traders were in town for ladies to go there without a man to protect them. The servant stayed with the sisters while Tía Dolores stepped inside a shop to trade Ana's blanket for boots for Juan and Antonio.

Patrick soon came up to the sisters to say hello. Even though it was very hot, Clara had been clutching her blanket tightly to her chest. But she handed it over without a murmur when Josefina and Francisca gave their blankets to Patrick.

"These are beautiful," said Patrick. "And they are

worth a great deal. Why are you giving them to me?"

Josefina took a deep breath. "We were wondering if you would consider taking them in trade for your— for your violin," she said all in a rush. That's what she said aloud. Inside she was praying, *Please let Señor Patrick say yes.*

Patrick looked surprised. "But I thought you wanted the little farm," he said to Josefina. "And you told me you wanted a mirror, Señorita Francisca. And you wanted knitting needles, Señorita Clara. You could get those things and more with these blankets."

"We *all* want the violin more than anything else," Josefina said firmly. "We want it for Papá."

"Ah!" said Patrick. He looked at the blankets and ran his hand over them. At last he said, "Your papá is very lucky to have daughters who love him so much. I'd be honored to trade my violin for blankets made by such good-hearted girls as you."

"Oh, gracias, Señor Patrick!" said Josefina with a huge smile.

"It's I who must thank you for these soft blankets," Patrick said. Then he added with a chuckle, "That violin isn't very comfortable to sleep on!"

Josefina laughed and Patrick went on to say, "Meet me here tomorrow afternoon at this same time. I'll give you the violin then."

"We'll be here!" promised Josefina and Francisca.

As Patrick walked away with their blankets, Clara shook her head. "I hope we can trust him," she said.

"Of course we can!" said Francisca stoutly. "Papá trusted him with the mules, didn't he?"

But Clara couldn't answer because Tía Dolores had returned. "Why, girls," she asked, "where are your blankets?"

"I hope you don't mind," said Francisca. "We traded them already."

Tía Dolores smiled. "What did you get?"

"Well," said Josefina. "We . . . it's . . ." Finally she gave up and grinned at her aunt. "We really can't say," she explained. "But you'll see tomorrow."

Tía Dolores laughed. "How nice!" she said. "You'll surprise me!"

"We certainly will," said Clara with a sigh.

But Josefina knew Clara was as excited about their surprise as she and Francisca were. Josefina was having a hard time hiding her own excitement. Her thoughts raced ahead to the next day. She couldn't *wait* to get the violin for Papá. She hoped the hours would fly by until it was time to meet Patrick!

Though it was raining hard the next afternoon, the three sisters went to the plaza with a servant to meet Patrick. They stood exactly where he had told them to be. They pulled their rebozos over their heads and hunched their shoulders against the rain. Hour after hour after hour the girls waited. By the time the bell in San Miguel Chapel rang for six o'clock prayers, their skirts were drenched and their shoes were sopping. It was clear that the servant was sorry he had come and was eager to go home where it was warm and dry. Josefina couldn't blame him. A gust of wind drove rain into her face so that it was as wet as if she had been crying.

"What shall we do?" asked Francisca. A strand of her hair was stuck flat against her cheek.

Clara shivered. "Let's go *home*," she said. "We've waited three hours. Señor Patrick is not coming. That's all. He's just not going to come."

"Maybe he forgot," said Josefina. "Maybe we misunderstood. Maybe we were supposed to come tomorrow."

"Maybe!" exclaimed Clara. "You can *maybe* all you want, but I'm going home right now! Abuelita will be worried sick about us."

"Wait!" said Josefina. She saw a man she knew was a friend of Patrick's. She gathered up all her courage and hurried to him. Clara and Francisca followed close behind. "Excuse me, señor," Josefina said. "Do you know where Señor Patrick O'Toole is?"

"Patrick O'Toole?" said the man. "He's gone."

Josefina's heart dropped. "But . . . but he was supposed to meet us here," she said. "There must be some mistake."

The man shrugged. "O'Toole's a scout," he said. "Last night, the captain of the wagon train told the scouts to head out for the Camino Real. By now they're long gone." The man nodded a brisk good-bye, then rushed off in the rain.

Gone! The word echoed inside Josefina's head. She felt as if she were in a cold, cruel nightmare. She stood numbly, too confused and miserable to talk.

Francisca was silent, too. But Clara had a lot to say. "I knew we shouldn't have trusted that Señor Patrick," she said furiously. "You know what this means, don't you? Señor Patrick has cheated us, so I'm sure he's cheated Papá, too! We've lost our blankets, but Papá has probably lost all the mules! We've got to get home to tell him."

"That's enough, Clara," said Francisca, her voice tired. She slid her arm around Josefina's shoulders. "Let's go."

Homeward the girls trudged. The wind swirled the rain around them. Josefina hardly noticed. She could think only of Patrick. With all her heart, she wanted to hold on to her trust in him. But it certainly seemed that Clara was right and that Patrick had lied to them all.

As they passed the toy trader, Josefina peered out from under her dripping rebozo and saw that the toy farm was gone. *Not that it matters,* Josefina thought sadly. *Now I have nothing to trade for it anyway.* But that was only a tiny disappointment compared to what Patrick seemed to have done. *Oh, Señor Patrick,* thought Josefina. *How could you betray us like this?*

Shining Like Hope

apá and Abuelito had gone to trade blankets for tools and did not come home until it was time for dinner. As soon as they walked in the door, Clara rushed to Papá. "Something terrible has happened," Clara said. "Señor Patrick is gone!"

"Gone?" gasped Abuelito. "But he hasn't paid your papá the rest of the silver he owes him. He promised—"

"Señor O'Toole's promises are lies," said Clara. "Yesterday Francisca, Josefina, and I gave him our blankets. He was supposed to meet us today to give us something in return for them. But he took our blankets and left! He stole them!" Clara looked at Papá and said, "He cheated us, so I'm certain he's cheated you, too."

"I knew it was a mistake to trust that americano!" said Abuelita. "He used his jokes and flattery and music to trick us into liking him! We didn't really know him at all!" She turned to Papá. "If you go to town right now, perhaps you can find your mules and get them back," she said.

Papá's face looked hard as stone.

Tía Dolores spoke carefully. "It's still possible that this is just a misunderstanding," she said. "If you reclaim your mules, you'll be saying that Señor Patrick is dishonest. If you're wrong, you'll shame him and yourself. You'll ruin his good name and your own as well."

"Sí," said Abuelito. "The other americanos won't want to trade with you, and you'll get nothing for your mules this year. You'd better be sure—"

"Sure?" interrupted Abuelita. "How much more sure could anyone be?" She spoke to Papá with urgency. "Señor O'Toole stole from your daughters. If he'd stoop to that, you can be sure he stole from you, too! Go now, get your mules back before the rest of the americanos leave, before it's too late!"

Papá was a wise man who did not act hastily. He thought for a long moment. Then he spoke in a sad, tired voice. "It seems I have been wrong to trust young

Señor O'Toole," he said. "I don't want to ruin my chances of trading with the other americanos, but I can't risk losing twenty good mules. I must do what I can to get them back."

"Sí!" began Abuelita. "Go—"

But Papá held up his hand. "It's useless to go now," he said. "It will be impossible to find the mules in the dark. I'll go tomorrow, at first light."

Abuelita pressed her lips into a thin, worried line and said no more. No one had any more to say. Soon after dinner, they all went to bed.

But Josefina was too miserable to sleep. For hours she lay awake, staring out of the narrow window. Finally she gave up. She rose, dressed, slipped outside, and climbed the hilltop behind the house.

The rain had washed the air clean, and the full moon was bright, shining like hope in the sky. Suddenly, out of the corner of her eye, Josefina saw a shadow move. "Señor Patrick?" she whispered, thinking wildly that he had come to find her.

But no. It was only an old tortoise making its way patiently across the sandy ground. Josefina sighed, and watched the tortoise stop under a piñón tree. Oddly,

the ground looked white there. Josefina looked again.
The ground wasn't white. Someone had left a piece of
paper under the tree. Josefina bent down to look at the
paper and gasped. *On top of the paper she saw Patrick's
chunk of turquoise!*

With trembling hands, Josefina picked up the turquoise and the paper. She unfolded the paper carefully,
knowing that Patrick must have left it for her. It was
soggy from being in the rain. The ink had run so much
that the drawing was blurry. When Josefina held it up
so that the moon shone on it, she could see that it was
a drawing of a church. But which church? There were
five in Santa Fe.

Was this one of Patrick's jokes? Josefina looked at
the chunk of turquoise and remembered how Patrick
had joked that it was a piece of the sky that fell into
his hand when he climbed to the top of . . . Oh!
Josefina pulled in her breath. San Miguel Chapel! That
was it! Patrick had left the chunk of turquoise on top
of the paper so that she would know that the drawing
was San Miguel Chapel. Josefina's heart skipped
a beat. That was where the violin was! Josefina
squeezed her fist shut around the piece of turquoise.

Oh, Señor Patrick! she thought. *Forgive me for thinking that you lied.*

Josefina slipped and slid down the rain-slick hill, tripping over her own feet in her hurry. She crossed the courtyard and burst into the room she shared with Francisca and Clara. "Wake up!" she hissed, shaking her sisters' shoulders. When they opened their eyes, Josefina waved the drawing at them and said, "Señor Patrick didn't lie! He left this to tell me where the violin is." She swallowed to catch her breath. "He left the violin in San Miguel Chapel."

"Let me see that," said Francisca. She lit a candle and took the drawing.

Clara looked bewildered. "But why . . ." she began.

"Señor Patrick put the violin in San Miguel Chapel because he knew it would be safe there," explained Josefina. "He had to leave Santa Fe in the middle of the night. He couldn't bring the violin here and wake up the whole household. He couldn't leave it up on the hilltop where it would be ruined by rain. He couldn't write a note to tell us where it was because we can't read English and he can't write Spanish. So he left me the drawing and his chunk of turquoise. He trusted me to figure it out." Josefina took the paper back from Francisca. "I'll show this to Papá, and it will prove to him that Señor Patrick is honest. Papá won't have to break off the trade!"

"Don't bother Papá with that! It's just a piece of paper," said Clara. "It doesn't prove anything. Only the violin would prove that Señor Patrick didn't cheat us— and Papá, too."

"Then I'll have to *get* the violin, won't I?" said Josefina. "I'll go now."

Clara was horrified. "Josefina!" she sputtered. "You can't go into Santa Fe by yourself in the middle of the night! It's dangerous. The traders drink too much. They gamble and fight and shoot off their guns." She shuddered. "You can't go."

"Not by yourself," said Francisca. She stood up and began to pull on her clothes. "I'll go with you."

"Oh, gracias, Francisca!" said Josefina. "We'll have to hurry. It'll be sunrise in a few hours. We've got to get the violin before Papá goes to town to take his mules back." She looked at Clara. "You must promise you won't tell anyone that we've gone."

"I promise," said Clara. "But *you* must promise to

be careful. I'll pray for you." She sighed. "If only I'd traded my blanket for those knitting needles!"

Josefina and Francisca crept from their room, tip-toed across the courtyard, and slid out the front gate. They sidled along the outside wall of the house. Then they darted to the kitchen garden and crouched behind its stick fence to catch their breath.

In a moment, Francisca touched Josefina's shoulder and then pointed toward the road. Josefina nodded. Both girls sprang forward, dashed to the road, and ran down it as fast as they could. With every step, the lantern she'd brought banged against Josefina's leg. Soon her arm ached from carrying it. Her stomach was in a knot, and her chest was burning because she was out of breath. But she kept on. Francisca was right by her side.

Soon light shining from windows and doorways spilled across the road. The girls heard bursts of music and clapping and the thunder of dancing feet com-ing from *fandangos* and parties. "We'll have to stay away from the plaza," whispered Josefina as she and

Francisca skittered down a narrow lane. "Too many people."

Francisca nodded. "Let's—" she began.

But just at that moment, the girls heard voices. A group of men swayed toward them, singing and laughing and all talking at once.

Quickly, Josefina and Francisca shrank into a doorway, pushing themselves flat against the door, holding their breath. Josefina's heart was pounding so loudly, she felt sure the men would hear it! But the rowdy men lurched by the girls' hiding place. Their voices filled the lane and then faded as they moved farther away. When she thought the men were gone, Josefina lifted her lantern and cautiously looked out to see if anyone else was coming. When she didn't see anyone, she signaled to Francisca to follow her.

But the moment the girls stepped out of the doorway, a rough voice frightened them. "What have we here?" said the voice. It belonged to a tall man who loomed toward them out of the darkness. "Two señoritas!" growled the man. He stepped forward, but Josefina tripped him, and he fell with a heavy thud. Josefina took hold of Francisca's hand and the two girls

ran for all they were worth, not caring where they went
as long as it was *away*.

Like birds of the night, Josefina and Francisca
darted from shadow to shadow, skirting the center of
town and never stopping. Just when Josefina thought
she could not run another step, the moon-washed
front of San Miguel Chapel rose up before them into
the dark night sky. Up the steps they flew. Josefina
grasped the handle of one of the huge doors with both
hands and pulled it with all her strength. Slowly, the
door creaked open and the two breathless girls ran
inside.

Trembling, the girls walked forward. It was cold
inside the church, and at first it seemed darker than
outside. Josefina's lantern made only a small circle of
light around her feet. But as her eyes adjusted, Josefina
saw candles placed in a cluster on the floor in front of
the altar where people had lit them and left them as
a kind of prayer. The candles shone like stars fallen
from the sky. With careful steps, Josefina and Francisca
walked toward them.

Suddenly, Josefina's heart soared up with happiness. For there, safely placed against the wall by a

small altar, was Patrick's violin in its case. *God bless you, Señor Patrick!* Josefina thought. She grabbed Francisca's hand and pulled her over to the violin. "Look!" she breathed. Patrick had even tied a ribbon around the violin case. Josefina knelt down and grinned. "I think Señor Patrick knew that you would come with me," she said to Francisca. Because next to the violin was the mirror that Francisca had wanted to get with her blanket.

Francisca smiled her beautiful smile. "He left something for you, too," she said. She picked up a small box and handed it to Josefina.

Josefina looked inside, and the first thing she saw was the funny pink pig. It was the little farm! All of the pieces fit together neatly in the small box. Josefina touched the farmhouse. *Gracias, Señor Patrick*, she thought. *I promise I will remember you every time I play with the little farm.*

"We'd better go," said Francisca.

The girls stood. When Josefina picked up the violin, something poked her hand. Josefina looked. Patrick had used the ribbon to tie knitting needles for Clara to the back of the violin case!

Josefina and Francisca glanced at each other and smiled. But there was no time to lose. When the girls walked outside the church, a thin streak of gray above the mountains was already hinting that the sun would soon rise. Josefina knew that meant Papá was probably awake and getting ready to come into town. She and Francisca had to get home fast. They had to stop him!

Though they were tired, Josefina and Francisca pushed themselves homeward as fast as they could go. The road home had never been so long.

As they ran toward Abuelito's house, they saw that they were just in time. Papá and Tía Dolores were standing together. Papá's horse was saddled, and he was just about to mount up to ride into town.

Josefina didn't hesitate. She ran straight to Papá and held out the violin. "Look, Papá," she said, all out of breath. "This is Señor Patrick's violin. This is what we traded our blankets for. He didn't lie to us. He left the violin for us in the church. Please don't go into town! Please don't take back your mules. Señor Patrick is honest. The violin proves it!" She thrust the violin into Papá's hands. "If he kept his promise to us, then surely he'll keep his promise to you."

Papá was astounded. He looked at the violin and then at his two daughters.

Tía Dolores was the first to speak. "Do you mean to say that you two—" She broke off, as if the rest of her question were too unbelievable to ask. "You two went into Santa Fe by yourselves in the middle of the night to get this violin?"

Josefina and Francisca nodded. "We're sorry," said Josefina.

"But we had to prove to Papá that Señor Patrick is honest," Francisca added.

They all looked at Papá. "You stopped me from making a serious mistake, and I am grateful," he said in his deep and deliberate voice. "Now I am sure that somehow Señor Patrick will get me the money he owes me for the mules." He paused, then said, "Go inside. Your abuelita will have some sharp words to say to you when she finds out what you have done, and I . . ."

The girls hung their heads. They knew they deserved the scolding they expected. But all Papá said was, "I must ask a servant to unsaddle my horse. It seems I won't be going to town this morning after all."

Francisca and Josefina glanced at each other. Wasn't

Papá going to scold them any more than that? They didn't wait to see, but turned to go inside.

"Wait!" said Papá. He held the violin out to Josefina. "Take your violin."

"Oh!" said Josefina. "The violin isn't for us. It's for you, Papá."

"For me?" Papá asked. "Why?"

"Because," said Josefina, "it made you and Tía Dolores happy."

Papá looked at Tía Dolores, and Josefina saw something that *might* have been a smile pass between them.

That evening, a friend of Patrick's brought the rest of the silver to Papá. Josefina and Francisca had only a peek at the man as he was leaving after dinner. They'd had to spend the day in their room as punishment for sneaking into town. Abuelita said that they should pray for God's forgiveness and everyone else's as well. But then she hugged both sisters, so Josefina thought she wasn't *too* angry. Clara was so delighted with her new knitting needles that she kept Josefina and Francisca company and knit all day. Francisca amused them by using her mirror to make reflected sunlight dance on the walls and flit across their skirts like tiny gold birds. Josefina spent the time quietly playing with her toy farm. And so the day passed peacefully. Josefina was tired after her adventure. She went to bed early and fell into a dreamless sleep.

Something woke her in the middle of the night. It wasn't the moon, because the sky was cloudy. Josefina got out of bed and opened the door to feel the cool night breeze on her cheeks. A sound nearly too soft to be heard drifted on the breeze. Josefina had to hold her breath to hear it. She almost wasn't sure what the sound was. When she realized, she smiled. Papá was gently, very gently, playing an old Spanish song on his violin.

The breeze blew the clouds away, and suddenly the courtyard was full of moonlight. Josefina saw that she was not the only one awake and listening to Papá. Standing in the doorway to her room, humming Papá's song, was Tía Dolores.

Gifts and Blessings

J osefina and her family returned to their rancho, and soon summer turned into fall. Then winter came, and all of Josefina's world was dusted with white, glittering snow and full of the excitement of the holiday season.

Early on the morning of January sixth, a whisper tickled Josefina's ear. "Josefina," it said. "Wake up."

Josefina was as cozy as a bird in its winter nest. But she pushed back her blanket and opened her sleepy eyes. She saw her little nephews, Juan and Antonio, crouched next to her. They were so close that she could feel their warm breath on her cheek and she could see, even in the darkness, that their faces were bright with excitement.

"Look!" whispered Juan. He and Antonio held up their shoes to show Josefina. "The three kings were here! They put treats in our shoes!"

"Yours, too, Josefina!" said Antonio, with a mouth full of sweets.

"Oh!" breathed Josefina. She sat up quickly and Antonio handed her one of her own shoes. In it, wrapped up in a scrap of clean cloth, there were pieces of candied fruits, slices of dried apples and apricots, and a small cone of sugar. Far down in the toe of her shoe there was a tiny goat carved out of wood that looked just like her pet, Sombrita.

January sixth was *La Fiesta de los Reyes Magos,* the Feast of the Three Kings. The night before, the children had followed an old tradition. They'd filled their shoes with hay and left them outside. The story was that the three kings would pass by on their way home from bringing gifts to the Christ Child in Bethlehem. The kings' camels would eat the hay, and the kings would leave sweets and gifts in the children's shoes to say thank you.

"The three kings were very generous to us," said Josefina as she nibbled a piece of candied melon.

Antonio sighed and Josefina saw that his shoe was already nearly empty. "My shoe's too small," he said, forgetting to speak softly.

"Shh!" shushed Juan. Josefina shared her sleeping sala with Clara and Francisca. Everyone knew that Francisca was grouchy all day if awakened too early. "Antonio, you had lots of sweets," whispered Juan, who was five. "You ate them too fast!"

Antonio hung his head. Josefina felt sorry for him. After all, he was only three. This was the first year he'd put his shoe out. Josefina remembered very, very well how it felt to be the youngest and to have the smallest shoe and to be so excited that she ate up her sweets instead of saving them the way her older sisters did. All that had changed. Francisca and Clara considered themselves too grown up, so now Josefina was the oldest child in the family to put out her shoe. "You can have some of my sweets," she said to Antonio. "I need my shoe, anyway. I can't hop to the stream on one foot."

"Gracias," said Antonio. He popped one of Josefina's sweets in his mouth and hopped around the room, first on one foot and then on the other.

Josefina watched him as she neatly rolled up her sheepskin and blankets and propped her doll, Niña, on top. "You boys had better hop back to your room and get dressed," she said quietly. "There's lots to do to get ready for the *fiesta* tonight." There was always a big fiesta, or party, to celebrate the Feast of the Three Kings, which was the last day of the Christmas season.

Clara was awake by now. She opened the door and a blast of cold air as sharp as an icicle came through. Francisca groaned and pulled her blanket over her head. "It snowed in the night," Clara said. "If it starts again, there might not be any fiesta."

Antonio stopped hopping and Juan asked, "No fiesta?"

"Don't worry," said Josefina. Now that she was almost eleven, she didn't let Clara's unhappy predictions discourage her. "It's early yet. As soon as the sun comes up, the sky will be blue. I'm sure of it. Now go!" She shooed the boys back to the room they shared with their parents, Ana and Tomás. Then she pulled on an extra petticoat, warm socks, and her warmest sarape and headed to the stream.

Josefina fetched water for the household first thing every morning. She enjoyed going to the stream even on wintry days like this one because each day was different. Today fresh new snow squeaked under her feet. The noisy stream greeted her, rushing around rocks capped with snow, then curving away out of sight. Josefina knew that the old saying *El agua es la vida* was true. Water was life to the rancho. Nothing could grow without it. The stream flowed along as steadily as time and blessed the rancho as it passed.

Josefina filled her water jar with the stinging-cold water. She put a ring of braided yucca leaves on her head and then balanced the jar on top of it. She walked back up the path thinking about all the delicious foods for the fiesta that this water would be used to make. There would be bizcochito cookies, spicy chile stew, and warm turnovers stuffed with fruit. Best of all, there would be dark, sweet hot chocolate. Josefina's feet moved faster at the thought of it.

Papá met her halfway up the path. "Oh, it's my Josefina," Papá said as he fell into step alongside her. "I thought you were a sparrow flying up the hill toward me. You're in a hurry this morning."

"Sí, Papá," said Josefina, "because of the fiesta tonight."

"Ah!" said Papá. "Tía Dolores tells me that you're

going to play the piano at the fiesta. She says you have a gift for music."

Josefina blushed. "Tía Dolores is very kind," she said.

"Sí," agreed Papá. "She is." They walked a few steps and then he said, "I can remember when you'd have been much too shy to play music at a fiesta."

"I am worried about it," Josefina admitted. "I don't think I could do it at all if it weren't for Tía Dolores. She taught me the piece of music I'm going to play and we've practiced it a lot. It's a waltz. I'm hoping everyone will be so happy dancing that they won't notice my mistakes! I especially hope Tía Dolores will be dancing. No matter how flustered I get, if I can look up and see her dancing, I'll be fine. I'll pretend I'm playing only for her."

"I'll tell you what," said Papá. "I'll ask Tía Dolores to dance the waltz with me. Then you need not worry."

"Oh, will you, Papá?" asked Josefina.

"I promise," he answered.

When Josefina and Papá came to the house, they saw that everyone was up and beginning the day's work. Juan and Antonio were energetically sweeping the snow out of the center courtyard. Or at least Josefina guessed that's what they were *supposed* to be doing. Actually, they were using their straw brooms to swoop the snow up into the air. Then they stood with their heads tilted back so that they could catch snowflakes on their tongues.

"I suppose we should stop them," said Papá with a grin.

Josefina didn't want to. The swirling snow was pretty. It glittered as it caught the early morning sun.

"Oh, please don't," said Tía Dolores, smiling as she came from the kitchen. She had a bundle of twigs, which she added to the fire already burning in the outdoor oven called the *horno*. "Ana has everything running smoothly in the kitchen. But we were tripping over those boys. They would not stop pestering us for tastes of food. They must have asked for cookies twenty times! Ana sent them out here, and the longer they're not in the way, the better."

Papá laughed and Josefina's heart lifted, as it always did, to hear him. Josefina remembered how it was just after Mamá died. Back then Papá seldom laughed or smiled. She and her sisters had been crushed by sorrow, too.

Then Tía Dolores had come to stay with them. Josefina looked at her aunt laughing along with Papá and thought about the wonderful changes Tía Dolores had made. She'd taught Josefina and her sisters to read and write. She'd helped them weave blankets to sell and trade. She'd brought her piano to the rancho and taught Josefina to play. Many evenings Papá played his violin while Tía Dolores played her piano. The rancho was a different place because of Tía Dolores. Josefina thought the best change of all was that Tía Dolores had helped their family to be happy again— especially Papá.

"Come along, Josefina," Tía Dolores said now in her brisk way. "Ana needs that water in the kitchen."

"Sí," said Josefina, smiling to herself. One thing Tía Dolores had taught *everyone* on the rancho was her favorite saying: *The saints cry over lost time.*

No time was being lost in the kitchen! It was humming with activity. Ana, who was in charge, was making turnovers. Carmen, busy cooking as usual, was stirring a big copper pot full of stew. Tía Dolores helped Carmen set the pot on an iron trivet over hot coals from the fire. Francisca's sleeves were rolled up and she was kneading bread dough.

"Bless you, Josefina," said Ana. She took the water jar. "Please help Francisca. I want the dough to rise while we're at morning prayers. The horno should be hot enough to bake the bread after prayers."

Clara was kneeling on the floor, using the *mano* and *metate*. She put a handful of dried corn on the flat metate stone and crushed it with the mano stone, rubbing back and forth until the corn was ground into coarse flour.

"Clara," Josefina said as she took off her sarape, "it's sunny. There's not one snow cloud in the sky."

Clara shrugged. "Not yet," she said, crushing another handful of corn. Then Clara surprised Josefina by smiling. "It's not that I want to be discouraging," she explained. "I just think it's foolish to get your hopes up the way you always do, Josefina. You're bound to be disappointed."

"I can't help it," said Josefina. "My hopes seem to go up whether I want them to or not."

"Like this bread dough," joked Francisca. She

pressed her fists into the dough and pushed down. "No matter how I flatten it, it rises up again."

"Hope is a blessing," said Tía Dolores.

"Sí," agreed Ana as she put some turnovers on a plate. "I think it's good to keep trying and never give up."

Just then, Juan and Antonio stuck their heads in the door. "Please," Juan asked for the twenty-first time, "can we have some cookies now?"

"What was that you said about never giving up?" Josefina asked Ana. And suddenly the kitchen was full of laughter.

After morning prayers and breakfast, Josefina and Tía Dolores carried the fat loaves of bread dough outside. Josefina took the wooden door off the horno, and smoke from the fire inside rose up into the blue sky. Josefina and Tía Dolores shoveled out the hot coals and swabbed the inside of the horno clean. When they finished, Tía Dolores put a tuft of sheep's wool on a wooden paddle.

"Oh, Tía Dolores, may I do it?" asked Josefina.

"Certainly," said Tía Dolores.

She gave Josefina the paddle, and Josefina put it into the horno. When the sheep's wool turned a toasty brown, Josefina knew the horno was just the right temperature to bake the bread. Josefina used her finger to press the shape of a cross on the tops of the loaves as a reminder that all the earth's bounty was a gift from God. Then, as Tía Dolores watched, she carefully put the loaves into the horno and wedged shut the heavy wooden door.

"Well done!" said Tía Dolores.

"I can take them out at the right time, too," said Josefina, boasting a bit.

"Good for you!" said Tía Dolores. "You don't need my help with the bread at all anymore, do you? But maybe I *can* help you practice the music you're playing tonight."

"Oh, yes, please," said Josefina. They walked together toward the *gran sala*, where the piano had been moved for the fiesta. "I'll practice playing the waltz, and perhaps you'd like to practice dancing it."

"Gracias," said Tía Dolores, laughing. "But that won't be necessary. I plan to be sitting right next to you at the piano while you play."

Josefina stopped and looked at her aunt. "Oh, but Tía Dolores," she said seriously. "Papá is hoping you'll dance the waltz with him. He told me so. You wouldn't want to disappoint him, would you?"

Tía Dolores slipped her arm around Josefina's shoulders. "No," she answered just as seriously. "I would never want to disappoint your papá."

Josefina was sure there had never been a more beautiful night for a fiesta. The huge, cold, black sky was sprinkled with stars, and the ground was silvery because of the moonlight shining on the snow. In the center courtyard of the house, a line of little fires lit the way to the gran sala, the biggest and grandest room, which was used only for special times like this.

Inside the gran sala, candlelight caught the bright colors of the ladies' best dresses and glinted off the men's buttons. Josefina and Clara were too young to dance, but they were allowed to sit on the floor and watch. Francisca swung by with her partner, and Ana waved gaily as she danced past with Tomás. Josefina

saw stout Señora Sánchez and kindly Señora López
both dancing with their husbands, and stately, white-
haired Señor García dancing with his wife. The guests
were friends from the village or from nearby ranchos,
and Josefina had known them all her life. Somehow,
though, their familiar faces looked different tonight.
Perhaps it was the gentle glow of candlelight or just the
magic of happiness that made the ladies look so lovely
and the men look so handsome.

After a while, Clara nudged Josefina. "Time to play
your waltz," she said.

Josefina stood, smoothed her skirt, and straightened
her hair ribbon.

"You look fine," Clara said. Then she stood too
and said kindly, "I'll go with you. Come on." The two
sisters walked through the crowded room to the piano.
Josefina was pleased to see that Francisca and Ana
were waiting for her there. They smiled encouragingly
as she sat down.

Josefina had never played music in front of a large
group of people before. Her hands were trembling.
Then, out of the corner of her eye, she saw Papá bow
and hold out his hand to Tía Dolores. Josefina began

to play, and Papá and Tía Dolores began to dance.
Josefina had always liked the lilting rhythm of the
waltz: *one-two-three, one-two-three, one-two-three.* And
tonight the music seemed to spiral up, up, up in ever
more graceful swoops and swirls as she played. She
never took her eyes off Papá and Tía Dolores. It was as
if all the other dancers had faded away. Around and
around and around Papá and Tía Dolores whirled.
Tía Dolores danced so lightly in Papá's arms it seemed
as if the music were wind and she and Papá were birds
carried on it.

Around and around and around they danced.
Papá and Tía Dolores belong together, thought Josefina.
They love each other. With her whole heart, she was
sure of it. Ana, Francisca, and Clara were watching
Papá and Tía Dolores, too. Josefina knew that her
sisters were thinking the same thought she was. And
she knew they were wishing, just as she was, that the
dance would never end.

Sleet

he bad weather Clara had predicted came howling in the next day. The sky was hard, dark and gray, and sleet clattered and bounced on the roof of the gran sala. Tía Dolores and the sisters had gathered in the gran sala to dust and sweep so that the room could be closed up until the next fiesta. The day was dreary, but Josefina needed only to close her eyes to imagine the way the gran sala had glowed with candlelight the night before. She hummed the waltz to herself as she swept.

Papá came in with two servants. They were going to move the table and chairs back to their usual places and put Tía Dolores's piano back in the family sala.

"Wasn't it a lovely fiesta?" Josefina sighed, looking at the piano.

"You know, I used to think a fiesta was hardly

worthwhile," said Clara, sounding unusually cheery. "There's so much work to do to get ready and even more work afterward to clean up! But last night's fiesta was worth it."

"And just wait till you're old enough to dance," said Francisca, twirling around her broom. "Then you'll love fiestas as much as I do."

"Preparing for a fiesta used to overwhelm me," said Ana. "But Tía Dolores has taught me to enjoy it. Now I think it's a pleasure to cook food for our friends to share."

"You did a wonderful job," Tía Dolores said to Ana. "All of you did." She looked around at all the sisters. Josefina thought Tía Dolores's face looked pale, as if she had not slept well the night before. "I am proud of you."

Papá spoke up. "Tía Dolores is right," he said. "Thanks to your hard work, that was a fiesta we'll all remember with great pleasure."

"Gracias, Papá," said the sisters happily. Such praise from Papá and Tía Dolores was delightful indeed! They all went contentedly back to work.

Except for Tía Dolores. She asked, "Do you remember that when I first came here, I said I would stay as long as you needed me?" The sisters stopped sweeping and looked at her as she went on. "You've all learned to do your sewing and weaving and household tasks very well. And you all did so beautifully preparing for the fiesta yesterday! I can see that you don't need me the way that you used to. So . . . so I've written to my parents and asked them to come here and take me back to Santa Fe with them. I'm going home."

The room was completely silent. The sisters were stunned still. Josefina felt as if a drop of freezing sleet were running right down her spine. "But Tía Dolores, *this* is your home," she burst out. "We thought you were happy here with us!"

"I am," said Tía Dolores. Then she squared her shoulders and spoke firmly, as if she'd made up her mind after a long struggle with herself. "But it's time for me to leave."

Josefina turned to Papá. He looked as shocked as she felt. Surely he would say something to Tía Dolores! But Papá only bowed his head for a moment. When he looked up, his face was composed and grave. He left the room without saying a word.

Tía Dolores watched him go. Then she picked up

her broom and went back to work. But Josefina and her sisters stared after Papá, as if he alone had the answer to a question that was desperately important to them all.

The more she thought about it, the angrier Josefina was with herself. Bragging about how she could make bread! Showing off playing the piano! *No wonder Tía Dolores doesn't feel needed!* Josefina thought. The sleet had stopped, but it was still very windy and cold as Josefina walked to the goat pen to see Sombrita. "But I know how to make things right," Josefina said to the little goat as it chewed on the fringe of her sarape. "I'll start tomorrow."

The odd thing was that her sisters seemed to have hit upon the same idea. The next morning, Francisca spilled tea at breakfast. Josefina was quite sure she did it on purpose. Francisca was wearing Clara's sash instead of her own, and the sash was badly stained. Francisca and Clara had sharp words about it, bickering just as they used to in the days before Tía Dolores had come and taught them to get along. Later that morning, Clara, who seldom made mistakes, snarled the wool, and four rows of weaving had to be disentangled from the loom. Ana somehow forgot to put salt in the sauce, so dinner tasted terrible. Josefina made mistakes all day long. She burned some *tortillas*, dropped a basket in a puddle, forgot part of a prayer, sat on her best hat, and was all thumbs at her piano lesson.

That evening Tía Dolores and the sisters gathered in front of the fire in the family sala. Papá didn't join them. His violin lay neglected on top of the piano. *Papá might as well give the violin back to Patrick O'Toole,* thought Josefina with a sigh. *He'll have no pleasure in playing it if Tía Dolores leaves.*

No one had much to say. Then Clara dropped her ball of knitting yarn. She and Ana leaned forward at the same time to pick it up and knocked heads. Ana pulled back so quickly she jarred Francisca's elbow, and Francisca pricked her finger with her sewing needle. Francisca yelped, which startled Josefina so that she made an ink splotch on her paper.

Tía Dolores shook her head. "I see what you girls are up to," she said. "You're deliberately bungling things so that it'll seem as if you still need me. But it

won't work. And you'd better stop before one of you
sets your skirts on fire!"

She laughed, and the sisters had to laugh at themselves, too.

"But Tía Dolores," said Clara, "we *do* need you."
Sometimes Josefina was glad that Clara was so
straightforward.

"Sí," agreed Francisca. "Not just as a teacher, but
as part of our family."

"We were so unhappy and lost after Mamá died,"
said Ana softly. "And you made everything better."

"We need you because we love you," said Josefina.

"Bless you!" said Tía Dolores, not laughing anymore. "I love you, too. That will never change. But you
girls have come a long way toward healing from the
sorrow of your mamá's death, God rest her soul. Your
papá has come a long way, too. It's time for him to
marry again, to give his heart to someone. If I am here,
I'm afraid I may be in the way. That's why it's time for
me to go. That's why I *want* to go."

"Oh, but Tía Dolores!" said Josefina. "Papá—" But
Ana squeezed Josefina's arm to stop her. They all knew
it would be wrong for Josefina to finish her sentence

and say to Tía Dolores, "Papá loves *you*." Children did not say such things to adults.

"Besides," said Tía Dolores with her usual brisk-ness, "if I am going to start a whole new life for myself in Santa Fe, the sooner I begin, the better."

The sisters could not look at one another or at Tía Dolores. There was nothing more they could say to her.

There was, however, a great deal for Josefina, Francisca, and Clara to say to one another later when they were together in their sleeping sala.

"Maybe this cold, sleety weather will stop Tía Dolores's letter from getting to Santa Fe," said Josefina, listening to the wind whistling outside the door. "Then Abuelita and Abuelito won't come to take her away."

"Don't be silly," said Clara. "Sooner or later, Tía Dolores is going to leave. Didn't you hear her say that she *wants* to go?"

Things were always black and white for Clara, plain as a wintry landscape of bare trees and snow. But

Josefina saw glimpses of color even in the starkest view.

"I don't think it's that simple," Josefina said now. "I don't think Tía Dolores truly wants to leave. She loves us, and . . ." Josefina swallowed and went on boldly, "I think she loves Papá. He loves her, too, but she doesn't know it."

"That's right," said Francisca. She sighed dramatically. "How terrible to love someone and think he doesn't love you in return. No wonder Tía Dolores wants to leave. Her heart must ache every time she sees Papá."

"Heavens above!" groaned Clara. "What nonsense! Tía Dolores isn't so foolish."

Josefina spoke with great certainty. "I know that Tía Dolores would stay," she said, "if Papá—"

"Asked her to marry him," all three sisters finished together.

"Sí," said Josefina. "The truth is, I've hoped he would for a long time now."

"Well," said Clara calmly. "Papá and Tía Dolores would be a good, sensible match, and a practical one, too." All the girls knew it was not unusual for a man to marry his wife's sister after his wife died. The families already knew each other, and it kept their property together.

"If they do decide to marry, they shouldn't waste any more time about it," said Clara. "Neither one of them is getting any younger. Besides, it's always best to have a wedding in the winter so that it won't get in the way of planting or harvesting."

"Oh, Clara!" exclaimed Francisca. "How can you be so matter-of-fact? You're forgetting all the wonderful steps in courtship. First, Papá has to write a letter asking Abuelito for Tía Dolores's hand in marriage. Then Abuelito and Abuelita ask Tía Dolores if the proposal is acceptable to her. If it isn't, then to say no, Tía Dolores must give Papá a squash—"

"There'll be no squash in this case. I'm sure of it!" Josefina cut in.

"And don't forget the engagement fiesta," Francisca rattled on, "and the groom's gifts to the bride, and—"

"Stop!" interrupted Clara. "There's one thing you're both forgetting: There's nothing *we* can do about *any* of this."

Josefina refused to give up. "There must be *something*," she said.

"Children are not involved in such matters," said Clara flatly. "It would be absolutely improper for us to talk to Tía Dolores or Papá."

Clara was right, as usual. But that did not stop Josefina. She thought for a while, and then she said, "I know someone we could talk to."

"Who?" asked her sisters.

"Tía Magdalena," said Josefina. "After all, she is Papá's sister and oldest relative, and the most respected woman in the village."

"When?" asked Clara.

"I'm sure Tía Magdalena will come to see Abuelito and Abuelita while they're here," said Josefina. "We'll ask her to speak to Papá. Oh, now I'm *glad* Abuelito and Abuelita are coming! That will make it all happen faster."

Francisca and Clara threw back their heads and started laughing.

"What's so funny?" asked Josefina.

"You are!" said her sisters.

"You find the sweet in the sour," said Clara. "The warm in the cold."

"The soft in the hard," added Francisca. "And

the light in the dark."

"Every time!" Clara and Francisca ended together.

Josefina didn't mind her sisters' teasing. She could tell that now they too were eager for Abuelito and Abuelita to arrive.

They did not have to wait long. Abuelito and Abuelita arrived from Santa Fe only a few days later. And just as Josefina had expected, Tía Magdalena came up from the village to see them the very first afternoon.

Before, during, and after dinner, Josefina waited for a chance to speak to Tía Magdalena, but they were surrounded by family all the time. It was not polite for a child to draw an adult aside for private conversation. Josefina knew she'd just have to sit and watch and wait and listen and hope for a quiet moment. It was hard because she was bubbling over with secret excitement.

Juan and Antonio were excited, too. They loved to see their great-grandparents, Abuelito and Abuelita. The boys showed their happiness with their whole bodies, frisking and dancing about the family sala until Abuelita scooped up Antonio, held him on her lap, and sat Juan right beside her.

"These are the finest boys in New Mexico," Abuelita said to Ana. "I really think that they should be educated by the priests in Santa Fe. Juan is old enough, and Antonio will be soon."

"Sí," agreed Abuelito. "It's an exciting time we live in. It's important for the boys to be educated so they can keep up. The world changes so fast!"

"And not all the changes are good," said Abuelita. "So many americano traders are coming to New Mexico now, with their different manners and customs and language! Most of them don't even share our Catholic faith." She shook her head. "I fear our most precious beliefs will be lost if we don't do all we can to teach them to our children."

"Now, now," said Abuelito. "Not all the americanos are so bad." He turned to Papá. "Don't you agree?"

Papá nodded. "Señor Patrick O'Toole is an honest young man," he said. "I plan to continue trading mules and blankets to the americanos with his help. He's a good fellow. I look forward to seeing him soon when he passes by on his way home to Missouri."

Abuelito leaned forward. "Then you will be interested to hear my news," he said. "I've been invited to join Señor O'Toole's wagon train and travel with it to Missouri. And I've decided to go!"

Everyone gasped. Abuelito went on with a pleased expression on his face. "I'll travel with the wagon train over the Santa Fe Trail to Franklin, Missouri. Then I'll ride a steamboat to St. Louis! I'll bring goods to trade and arrange for goods to be sent back here. What an adventure it will be! I guess I'm not such an old man after all!"

"May God watch over you," said Tía Magdalena, who'd been listening silently.

Josefina was trying to imagine what a steamboat might look like when Abuelito said something that made her heart stop.

Abuelito smiled at Tía Dolores. "You know, my dear, I must thank you," he said. "I wasn't going to accept the invitation. I didn't want to leave your mother alone all the months I'd be away. But when we got your letter saying that you wanted to come home,

I knew I could say yes. Because you're coming home to
Santa Fe, I can go to Missouri with the americanos!"

Oh, no! thought Josefina. *This is terrible.*

Then it got worse. "I was glad to get your letter,
too, my daughter," said Abuelita to Tía Dolores. "Your
father and I have waited a long time for you to come
home to Santa Fe. It's such a comfort to know you'll be
living with us as we grow old."

"I'm glad to be needed," said Tía Dolores softly.

Needed! Josefina felt a door slamming shut when
she heard the word. She and Francisca and Clara
exchanged agonized looks. How could Papá ask
Tía Dolores to marry him *now*? It would seem selfish,
and it would hurt Abuelito and Abuelita. Tía Dolores
would never say yes if Papá *did* ask her. Her first duty
was to her parents. It would be unthinkable for her to
let them down.

Josefina could not bear to hear any more. Quietly,
she slipped out of the family sala, ran across the cold
courtyard, and went to her sleeping sala. It was dusk,
and the room was full of shadows. Josefina sat on the
floor, hugging her knees to her chest.

She was all alone for a few minutes. Then someone

came into the dark room and asked, "Josefina?"

It was Tía Magdalena.

Josefina jumped to her feet and stood, head bowed, in the respectful way children were supposed to stand in the presence of an adult.

Tía Magdalena sat on the *banco* and motioned Josefina to sit next to her on the bench. "All afternoon I've had the feeling that you wanted to ask me something," she said.

"Sí, Tía Magdalena," said Josefina. "I did. But . . . I beg your pardon, but I don't need to anymore."

"I see," said Tía Magdalena. But she didn't leave. Instead she said, "I've invited your Tía Dolores to stay with me for a few days before she goes to Santa Fe with her parents. I've grown so fond of her, and it'll be a long, long time before I see her again. Santa Fe's too far for me to travel anymore. Ah, well, we'll *all* miss your Tía Dolores very much when she leaves, won't we?"

Now the words spilled out of Josefina. "Oh, Tía Magdalena!" she said. "It will be terrible if Tía Dolores leaves. It will be the way it was just after Mamá died, when we were all so sad. We were . . ."

Josefina faltered. Gently, Tía Magdalena finished for her. "You were heartsick with sorrow," she said.

"Sí!" said Josefina. She spoke with conviction. "Tía Dolores mustn't leave! She belongs here! I was going to ask you to speak to Papá so that you could ask him to . . . to set it all straight." Josefina shook her head as she went on. "But now Abuelito and Abuelita need Tía Dolores in Santa Fe. She *has* to leave. There's nothing anyone can do."

"Dear child!" said Tía Magdalena. "I'm afraid you're right. Curanderas don't have medicine to heal such troubles."

Josefina sighed. There was one narrow window in the sleeping sala, and only a sliver of the twilight sky showed through. Josefina could see just one star, a tiny pinprick of light, shining very far away. "With all my heart," she said softly, "I want Tía Dolores to stay."

Tía Magdalena took Josefina's hand in hers. "Here," she said. She put something as smooth and cool as a raindrop into Josefina's palm.

It was so dark, Josefina had to lift her hand close to her eyes to see what Tía Magdalena had given her. It was a *milagro*, a little medal. Josefina knew that a

milagro was a symbol of a special hope or prayer.
When someone wanted to ask a saint for help, he'd
pin a milagro to that saint's statue. If he was praying
to find a lost sheep, he would choose a milagro in the
shape of a sheep. If he was praying for a hurt foot to
heal, he would choose a milagro in the shape of a foot.

"I want you to keep this milagro with you," said
Tía Magdalena. "It will remind you to pray for your
family's happiness, for your sorrow to be healed.
And perhaps it will help you not to lose hope in your
heart's desire."

"Gracias, Tía Magdalena," said Josefina. She looked
closer. The milagro Tía Magdalena had given her was
in the shape of a heart.

Josefina's Plan

arly the next morning, Tía Dolores left Papá's
rancho and went to Tía Magdalena's house
in the village, which was about a mile away.
It was a bleak day. The tree branches were coated
with hard, new ice, and they clinked when the wind
knocked them together.

All that day, Josefina thought that the rancho
seemed to be under a terrible spell, frozen in gloom,
even though everything ran smoothly enough. No
one spilled tea or ruined weaving or burned tortillas.
Dinner was well cooked and served on time. Josefina
did not make one single mistake when she practiced
playing the piano. And yet somehow, the music was
all wrong. It was just noisy, clanging sound. There was
no joy in it. Since the piano would soon be gone with
Tía Dolores, there didn't seem to be much point in

practicing anyway. There didn't seem to be much point in anything at all.

This is what it will be like forever after Tía Dolores leaves, thought Josefina sadly. She was wearing the heart milagro on a thread around her neck. Every time she moved, she felt the cool little heart touch her chest. She was grateful for its comfort. It was like a gentle voice saying, *Perhaps there's still hope. Perhaps there's a way Tía Dolores can stay. Perhaps tomorrow you'll think of something. . . .*

But the next day came and Josefina felt as dull as the weather. Fat gray clouds hung so low over the mountains that the snowy peaks poked through. Everyone seemed unhappy, except for Abuelita and Abuelito. Abuelito talked to Ana's husband, Tomás, about the new plow Tomás had bought from the americano traders and the new system of ditches Tomás and Papá had dug on the rancho to bring water to the fields.

"That Tomás is a clever fellow," Abuelito said to Abuelita. "He's not afraid of change. He did a fine job managing the rancho last summer while the rest of the family was in Santa Fe. I wish I had a manager who'd do as well for me while I'm away."

Josefina and Abuelita were in the family sala
playing clapping games with Juan and Antonio.
Abuelita looked at Abuelito and smiled. "Cleverness
runs in the family," she said. "Ana manages this
household as smoothly as any I've ever seen. And
I've never known two brighter boys than little Juan
and Antonio." She sighed and hugged the boys.
"Bless their dear hearts," she said. "How I shall miss
them when we leave! I wish I could watch them grow
and change!"

Josefina's brain seemed to wake up at that moment.
An idea started to take shape. She thought about it all
day, then presented her plan to Clara and Francisca
that night as they were getting ready for bed. They
sighed and shook their heads doubtfully when they
heard Josefina's idea.

But Josefina was determined. "We've got to *try*,"
she said.

So the next morning, Francisca, Clara, and
Josefina presented the plan to Ana. She spoke to
her husband, Tomás, and then all four sisters went
together to Papá.

Papá was in the family sala. He had a pen in his

hand and Tía Dolores's ledger book lying open in front
of him, but he was staring into the fire when the girls
came into the room.

The four sisters stood with their hands folded
and their heads bowed, waiting for Papá to acknowl-
edge them.

He turned and said, "Sí?"

"With your permission," said Ana, "we'd like to
speak to you, Papá."

"Sí," Papá said again.

Ana looked at Josefina, Clara, and Francisca. They
nodded to urge her to begin.

"Papá," said Ana respectfully. "Would you honor
us by considering an idea we have?" She paused. "Do
you think it might be possible for Tomás and our sons
and me to go to Santa Fe with Abuelito and Abuelita?"

Papá looked at the fire again as Ana went on.
"Tomás could manage Abuelito's rancho while Abuelito
is away on his trip to Missouri," she said. "I could keep
Abuelita company and help her run her household.
Juan could go to school and be educated by the priests.
And Antonio, well, he will be happy to be with his dear
great-grandmother who loves him so."

"Is this plan your idea?" Papá asked Ana.

"No," said Ana.

"It was Josefina's idea," said Clara.

Papá folded his arms across his chest and looked at Josefina. Then he asked Ana, "Is this what you and Tomás want?"

"Sí," answered Ana. "We'll be sad to leave here. But this would be a step forward for Tomás and our little family. I think it would be a good thing for Abuelito and Abuelita, as well. It would be good for you, too, Papá, and my sisters because—"

"Because then Tía Dolores would stay here!" Josefina ended.

Papá's face softened. His voice was gentle when he spoke. "I think this idea would be a wonderful thing for almost everyone," he said. "But I'm afraid that there is a problem with it. Tía Dolores has told us that she wants to leave our rancho and go to Santa Fe. If you go instead, Ana, she'll feel she's needed here to help run our household. It seems to me that all her life she's had to go where she was needed instead of where she wanted to go."

"But we don't believe that she really wants to go to

Santa Fe," Josefina blurted out. "It's just that she thinks she should. You could convince her to stay, Papá!" Josefina didn't come right out and say *If you asked her to marry you*, but that is what she meant.

"Dear child!" said Papá, smiling. "You have a great deal of faith in my ability to change Tía Dolores's mind!"

"Please, Papá," asked Ana. "May we ask you to think about our idea, and perhaps consider presenting it to Abuelito and Abuelita? They may have an opinion about it."

"I will consider it," said Papá. "You have my word."

"Gracias, Papá," said the sisters. Quickly, they left the room.

"I don't think that went very well," said Clara.

"He *said* he'd think about Josefina's plan," said Ana.

"But he has to do more than that," said Francisca. "He has to ask Abuelito and Abuelita for Tía Dolores's hand in marriage. She won't stay here if he doesn't."

"Well, he'd better do it soon," said Clara. "Tía Dolores will come back from Tía Magdalena's any day now. As soon as she does, she'll leave with Abuelita and Abuelito for Santa Fe."

"Oh, I hope Papá asks Tía Dolores to marry him," said Francisca.

"He will!" said Josefina. "I just know Papá will!"

Josefina's sisters couldn't help but smile at her.

"Josefina," said Ana in her gentle way. "Don't get your heart set on it."

"It's too late," Josefina said cheerfully. She patted the heart milagro. "My heart's been set on it for a long, long time already."

That very evening, when the family was gathered in front of the fire, Francisca jabbed Josefina to make her look up. Josefina tugged on Clara's skirt and Clara nudged Ana. All four sisters watched Papá hand Abuelito a folded piece of paper. They heard Papá ask Abuelito, "Would you do me the honor of reading this?"

"Of course!" said Abuelito. He and Papá and Abuelita left the room.

"Did you see that?" said Josefina joyfully. "Papá just gave Abuelito a letter asking for Tía Dolores's hand in marriage!"

"No, he didn't," said Clara. "The letter just presents the idea of Ana and Tomás and the boys going to Santa Fe."

Of course, there was no way of knowing who was right. But Josefina was sure she was, especially the next morning when she and Clara saw Abuelito and Abuelita setting out to walk to the village.

"Oh!" exclaimed Josefina, hugging Clara in her excitement. "Abuelita and Abuelito are going to ask Tía Dolores if she accepts Papá's marriage proposal!"

"No," said Clara. "They're just going to ask Tía Dolores how she feels about your plan. If she wants to go to Santa Fe, then Ana and Tomás won't go."

It was a blustery day and the whole sky was a pale, ghostly white, as if the clouds were full of snow waiting, waiting, waiting to fall. Josefina and her sisters were waiting, waiting, waiting, too, for Abuelita and Abuelito to come back from the village. Josefina came up with a hundred excuses to go outside and look down the road to see if she could spot them returning.

"What could they be doing?" she fussed to her sisters. They were in the kitchen preparing the mid-day

meal. A stick hung crossways in front of the hearth
with dried squash and garlic and chiles dangling from
it. Josefina tapped the stick to make the vegetables
jiggle, as if they felt the same jittery impatience that she
did. "Why is this taking so long? All Tía Dolores has
to do is say yes or no!"

"*If* they're talking about marriage," said Clara,
"which they're not."

Ana tried to soothe things. "Abuelito and Abuelita
have many friends in the village," she said. "Their
friends have probably come to Tía Magdalena's house
to visit with them. And I suppose that Abuelito has
told them that he's going to Missouri with the americanos, so they all have a lot to say. I'm sure everyone is
surprised."

"Oh!" exploded Josefina. "In another minute I'll run
to the village myself to see what is going on!"

"Heavens!" said Clara rather primly. "You can't do
that. Remember, this is none of our business. Children
are not involved in such things."

Francisca rolled her eyes at Josefina and grinned.
They knew that Clara was really every bit as curious as
they were, though she liked to hide it.

It was late afternoon before Abuelito and Abuelita returned from the village, just in time for evening prayers. After prayers, as they all walked out into the courtyard, Abuelito turned to Papá.

"Well, Dolores surprised us," Abuelito said. The sisters were hardly breathing so that they could hear every word. "We discussed the idea of Ana and Tomás coming to Santa Fe instead of her."

Clara gave Josefina a look that said, *I told you so.*

Josefina's heart sank. So Clara had been right. Papá's letter had *not* been a proposal of marriage. *Oh, Papá!* thought Josefina, bitterly disappointed.

Disappointment turned to horror and disbelief when Abuelito went on to say, "Dolores thinks that Francisca and Clara and Josefina are perfectly capable of running this household without her help *or* Ana's! She says it's time for her to leave even if Ana leaves too. She's coming to Santa Fe no matter what Ana and Tomás do. So we'll pack up her belongings tomorrow, and we'll leave the day after."

"Very well," said Papá in a low, even voice.

No! Josefina wanted to shout out loud. *No!* Tía Dolores leaving *and* Ana leaving? That's not at all what was supposed to happen! Oh, how could her plan have turned out so badly? Hot tears filled Josefina's eyes. With a rough yank, she broke the thread with the heart milagro on it. She flung the milagro onto the slushy ground and walked away.

Heart and Hope

 hen Mamá died, Josefina had thought that the world should stop. It had seemed wrong to carry on with everyday chores, as if nothing had changed. But over time, she had learned that work was a great comfort in hard times. It was a blessing to do simple tasks like cooking and washing and sweeping, tasks that had to do with hands, not hearts.

Josefina felt that way the next morning. She was glad to go out into the biting cold to fetch water from the stream. She was glad the water jar was heavy and the hill was steep as she trudged back to the house. She was glad her heart pounded in her chest from the hard work, else she'd think it had withered from sadness. When Mamá died, Josefina had thought she could never feel that sad ever again. Now she knew she'd been wrong.

Papá met Josefina halfway up the hill, just as he had on the morning of the fiesta. But this morning, they walked in silence. They'd almost reached the house when Papá stopped. He reached into his pocket. "Josefina," he asked, "I found this in the courtyard last night. Is it yours?"

Josefina put her water jar on the ground and looked. She saw something muddy dangling from Papá's hand. It was the heart milagro. Josefina frowned. "It was mine," she said. "But I don't want it."

Papá held the milagro in his hand and wiped the mud off it with his finger. "I suppose there's nothing harder to give someone than a heart she doesn't want," he said slowly. "Tell me why you don't want this one."

"Tía Magdalena gave it to me," Josefina explained. "She said it would remind me to pray for our family's happiness, for our sorrow to be healed. And . . ." Josefina sighed, remembering. "She said it would help me not to lose hope in my heart's desire."

"I see," said Papá. The day's very first ray of sun peeked over the mountaintop and between two clouds. Papá tilted his hand so that, just for a second, sunlight found the milagro and made it shine. When he spoke, Josefina knew that he was trying to comfort her. "I know what your heart's desire was, Josefina," he said. "When you and your sisters came to me with your plan, I knew what you were thinking. You wanted to make it possible for me to ask Tía Dolores to stay here as my wife. That would have made you happy. And it would have made me happy, too."

Josefina looked at Papá with a question in her eyes. But he was looking up at the mountains, so he didn't see.

"The simple truth is that we can't always have what we hope for in life," Papá said. "Tía Dolores told us that she wants to leave, and so we mustn't stop her. When we love someone, *especially* when we love someone, we must let her go if she wants to go. We must put her heart's desire before our own." Papá turned to Josefina. "Do you understand?" he asked gently. "We want Tía Dolores to be happy, don't we?"

"Oh, but Papá!" said Josefina desperately. "Tía Dolores doesn't want to leave. She thinks she should, for *your* happiness. She said that it's time for you to give your heart to someone, and she's in the way."

Then Josefina gathered up all her hope and courage and told the truth straight out. "Don't you see, Papá?" she said. "Tía Dolores loves you. That's why she *can't* stay. Because she thinks that you don't love her in return."

Papá shook his head and looked away from Josefina.

It's no use, thought Josefina. She lifted the water jar back onto her head and started to walk up the hill to the house.

"Josefina!" Papá called after her. "Do you want your milagro?"

Josefina turned. The heart milagro looked very, very small in Papá's hand. "No thank you, Papá," she said. "It's yours now."

Josefina did not see Papá again until the mid-day meal.

"Josefina," said Papá. "Your grandparents are walking to the village this afternoon. They're going to bring Tía Dolores back here. I want you to go along to help."

"Sí, Papá," said Josefina, even though there was no walk in the world she dreaded more. She had no desire to help Tía Dolores begin to leave them!

Josefina, Abuelito, and Abuelita set forth for the village under a winter sun so pale it didn't warm the air at all. Josefina's nose hurt and her mouth had the bitter taste of cold in it. A mean wind made her eyes water, so she bent her head forward and pulled down the brim of her hat.

"Brrr!" shivered Abuelito. "That wind cuts through me! My hands are frozen stiff." He glanced at Josefina. "My child," he said. "Put this paper in your pouch and carry it for me." Abuelito handed Josefina a folded paper and she put it in a leather pouch that hung from a string around her neck. "Gracias," said Abuelito. He rubbed his hands together to warm them. "Oh, how glad I'll be to get to your Tía Magdalena's house and stand in front of her fire!"

They were *all* glad to come into the warmth of Tía Magdalena's house. A cheerful fire crackled on the hearth, and steam rose in a cloud from a big kettle. Tía Dolores smiled at Josefina, and Tía Magdalena helped Abuelita sit next to the fire. "Come! Sit and be comfortable," Tía Magdalena said. "You must have a cup of tea."

"Gracias," said Abuelita. "You are very kind."

When they were settled, Abuelito said, "Josefina, please give me the paper." Josefina took the folded paper out of her pouch and handed it to Abuelito. He gave it to Tía Dolores, saying, "A letter for you, my dear."

As Tía Dolores unfolded the letter, something fell onto her lap. It was small and shiny and bright as a spark in the firelight. "Why, what's this?" asked Tía Dolores, holding the little object in her fingertips and looking at it curiously.

Josefina gasped. *It was the heart milagro!* Suddenly, Josefina knew. The letter was a proposal from Papá! She was so happy, she wanted to jump up and shout for joy. "It's a heart!" she exclaimed. "It's Papá's! He's giving it to you. Oh, please read the letter, Tía Dolores! Then you'll see."

Tía Dolores began to read the letter, and her eyes grew wide. "Oh!" she exclaimed softly. Then, "Oh," she said again.

Everyone sat perfectly still, watching Tía Dolores.

When she finished reading, Tía Dolores looked at
Abuelito and Abuelita, and her face was lit with pure
happiness. "Well," she said finally in a voice that trem-
bled a little. "Josefina's papá has done me the honor of
asking for my hand in marriage. Please tell him that
my answer is yes."

"Bless you, my child!" exclaimed Abuelito. "We
will."

Josefina jumped up and threw her arms around
Tía Dolores's neck. She could feel Tía Dolores's happy
tears on her own cheek.

On the day that Papá and Tía Dolores were to be
married, the sun shone down on snow as white as new
milk and dazzled the world with light. And yet the air
carried a wisp of softness. Josefina took a deep breath
as she walked up the hill from the stream. There was
no mistaking the teasing hint of spring. She smiled to
herself, thinking of the sprouts still sleeping under the
snow, soon to be awakened by the spring sun.

This morning, both Papá and Tía Dolores met
Josefina partway up the path to the house from the

stream. They stood together, smiling, as they waited for Josefina to draw near.

"Josefina," said Papá. "Tía Dolores and I want you to do something."

Tía Dolores pulled Josefina's hand toward her and put the heart milagro in it. "This is rightly yours," she said, "because you never forgot your heart's desire."

"Will you keep the heart milagro safe for us?" asked Papá, smiling at Josefina with love.

"I will," said Josefina. "I promise."

Josefina remembered her promise later. She held the heart milagro in her hand as she stood outside the church after the wedding ceremony. Everyone she loved most dearly was gathered around her. Brave Abuelito, who was about to set forth on a new adventure. Dignified Abuelita, who held her chin up as if she were wearing a crown. Tía Magdalena, whose kindness and wisdom never failed her. Sweet Ana, her devoted Tomás, and their lively boys. Headstrong Francisca and sensible Clara. Josefina was sure that Mamá was there, too, in everyone's thoughts.

Villagers and neighbors, workers from the rancho, and friends from the pueblo cheered Papá and

Tía Dolores, who smiled and waved. Musicians struck up a lively tune, and the church bell rang out joyously. A flock of birds, startled by the sound, rose up with a great exuberant fluttering of wings. Josefina smiled. She knew just how those birds felt. Her heart rose up with them into the endless blue sky.

INSIDE Josefina's World

For more than 200 years, New Mexican settlers lived as the Montoyas did. But when Josefina was a girl, a time of great change was beginning for New Mexico.

The changes started in 1821, the year that Mexico won independence from Spain. Until then, foreigners were not allowed to do business in New Mexico. But after 1821, American traders began traveling to Santa Fe from Missouri. The wagon trail they took was called the Santa Fe Trail. Within just a few years, dozens of American wagon trains were coming to Santa Fe every summer.

The flood of American goods began to affect the way New Mexicans dressed, did their chores, and decorated their homes. By the time Josefina was a mother, she might have had glass windows, wallpaper, and some American-style furniture. By the time she was a grandmother, she might have given up practical New Mexican–style clothes and started to wear corsets, hoopskirts, and bonnets.

Many Americans of the time looked down on Mexican people or made fun of customs they did not understand. Still, people in the United States saw opportunity in the Mexican lands to the southwest, and they began to feel that these lands should belong to the U.S.

In December 1845, the U.S. government tried to buy Mexico's northern lands. When Mexico refused to sell, the U.S. declared war. American soldiers arrived in Santa Fe in August 1846 and established American rule there without any fighting. Some New Mexicans welcomed the change, but others feared that their way of life and most precious traditions would soon be lost.

The Mexican War was fought farther south and west until 1848. By then, the U.S. had taken almost all the land that is now New Mexico, Arizona, California, Nevada, Utah, and Colorado. Everyone living there, except Native Americans, was granted U.S. citizenship. Josefina would have become an American when she was 33 years old.

After the war, more and more Americans came from the East, including missionaries, cattle ranchers, miners, and outlaws. Some native New Mexicans suffered great losses as a result. Many families lost valuable land they had owned for 200 years or more, or lost precious rights to use water for irrigating their fields. The Apache and Navajo tribes were forced onto reservations.

In the 1880s, as railroads began bringing tourists and artists to the Southwest, Americans started to develop greater appreciation for New Mexico's landscape, climate, and cultures. New Mexico and Arizona were granted statehood in 1912.

New Mexicans learned to take part in American life. But they also worked to hold on to their cultures—their faith, language, beliefs, arts, foods, and other traditions. Today the Southwest is a vital and unique part of the United States that reflects the rich cultural traditions of all the people who call it home.

GLOSSARY of Spanish Words

Abuelita *(ah-bweh-LEE-tah)*—Grandma

Abuelito *(ah-bweh-LEE-toh)*—Grandpa

acequia *(ah-SEH-kee-ah)*—a ditch made to carry water to a farmer's fields

adiós *(ah-dee-OHS)*—good-bye

adobe *(ah-DOH-beh)*—a building material made of earth mixed with straw and water

americano *(ah-meh-ree-KAH-no)*—a man from the United States

banco *(BAHN-ko)*—a bench built into the wall of a room

bienvenido *(bee-en-veh-NEE-doh)*—welcome

bizcochito *(bees-ko-CHEE-toh)*—a kind of sugar cookie flavored with anise

buenos días *(BWEH-nohs DEE-ahs)*—good morning

Camino Real *(kah-MEE-no rey-AHL)*—the main road or trail that ran from Mexico City to New Mexico. Its name means "Royal Road."

curandera *(koo-rahn-DEH-rah)*—a woman who knows how to make medicines from plants and is skilled at healing people

doña *(DOH-nyah)*—a term of respect for an older woman

El agua es la vida. *(el AH-gwah es lah VEE-dah)*—a traditional New Mexican saying that means "Water is life." It shows how important water is to people living in a desert climate.

fandango *(fahn-DAHNG-go)*—a big celebration or party that includes a lively dance

fiesta *(fee-ES-tah)*—a party or celebration

gracias *(GRAH-see-ahs)*—thank you

gran sala *(grahn SAH-lah)*—the biggest room in the house, used for special events and formal occasions

horno *(OR-no)*—an outdoor oven made of *adobe*, or earth mixed with straw and water

inmortal *(een-mor-TAHL)*—a plant called "spider milkweed" in English. It can be used to make a medicine for colds.

La Fiesta de los Reyes Magos *(la fee-ES-tah deh lohs REY-es MAH-gohs)*—the Feast of the Three Kings. This is the Catholic feast day that celebrates the Bible story of the three wise men bringing gifts to the baby Jesus.

mano *(MAH-no)*—a stone that is held in the hand and used to grind corn. Dried corn is put on a large flat stone called a *metate*, and then the mano is rubbed back and forth over the corn to break it down into flour.

manzanilla *(mahn-sah-NEE-yah)*—a plant known as "chamomile" in English. It can be used to make a soothing tea.

metate *(meh-TAH-teh)*—a large flat stone used with a *mano* to grind corn

milagro *(mee-LAH-gro)*—a small medal that symbolizes a request that a person is praying for or a prayer that has been answered

piñón *(pee-NYOHN)*—a kind of short, scrubby pine that

produces delicious nuts

plaza *(PLAH-sah)*—an open square in a village or town

por favor *(por fah-VOR)*—please

pueblo *(PWEH-blo)*—a village of Pueblo Indians

rancho *(RAHN-cho)*—a farm or ranch where crops are grown and animals are raised

rebozo *(reh-BO-so)*—a long shawl worn by girls and women

sala *(SAH-lah)*—a room in a house

San Miguel *(sahn mee-GEHL)*—Saint Michael

Santa Fe *(SAHN-tah FEH)*—the capital city of New Mexico. Its name means "Holy Faith."

sarape *(sah-RAH-peh)*—a warm blanket that is wrapped around the shoulders or worn as a poncho

señor *(seh-NYOR)*—Mr. or sir

señora *(seh-NYO-rah)*—Mrs. or ma'am

señorita *(seh-nyo-REE-tah)*—Miss or young lady

sí *(SEE)*—yes

sombrita *(sohm-BREE-tah)*—little shadow, or an affectionate way to say "shadow." The Spanish word for "shadow" is *sombra*.

tía *(TEE-ah)*—aunt

tortilla *(tor-TEE-yah)*—a kind of flat, round bread made of corn or wheat

Read more of JOSEFINA'S stories,

available from booksellers and at *americangirl.com*

⚜ *Classics* ⚜

Josefina's classic series, now in two volumes:

Volume 1:
Sunlight and Shadows

Josefina and her sisters are excited when Tía Dolores comes to their *rancho*, bringing new ideas, new fashions, and new challenges. Can Josefina open her heart to change and still hold on to precious memories of Mamá?

Volume 2:
Second Chances

Josefina makes a wonderful discovery: She has a gift for healing. Can she find the courage and creativity to mend her family's broken trust in an *americano* trader and keep her family whole and happy when Tía Dolores plans to leave?

⚜ *Mystery* ⚜

Another thrilling adventure with Josefina!

Secrets in the Hills

Josefina has heard tales of treasure buried in the hills, and of a ghostly Weeping Woman who roams at night. But she never imagined the stories might be true—until a mysterious stranger arrives at her rancho.

⊶ A Sneak Peek at ⊷

Secrets
in the Hills

A Josefina Mystery

Josefina's adventures continue
in an exciting mystery.

osefina stared at Señor Zamora, who was tucked into bed like a child. His forehead glistened with sweat, and he was mumbling under his breath. "What is he saying?"

Tía Dolores shook her head. "He's not making sense. That can happen with high fevers. Will you fetch more water, please? I'll have his leg bandaged by the time you return."

Josefina saw Señor Zamora's face in her mind as she hurried to the stream with a water jar. She had been worried about tending Doña Felícitas in the village— and now a patient with more serious problems had appeared! Had the mysterious stranger been sent to test her skill and knowledge?

As Josefina returned to the sala, she heard Tía Dolores talking to Señor Zamora in a soothing tone. "Your things are safe here, señor."

"Is his mind clearer?" Josefina asked, putting the water jar by the bed.

Tía Dolores shook her head. "Not really. He seems to be worried about his clothes." She gestured to a pile by the door. "Miguel provided our guest with a clean shirt to wear."

"We should put a damp cloth on his forehead," Josefina said. "That will help bring his fever down."

"You go ahead," Tía Dolores said. "I need to make sure that dinner preparations are well in hand. I'll return in a moment."

Josefina poured water into a bowl, wrung out a cloth, folded it neatly, and draped it over her patient's forehead. His eyes opened for a moment, as if he was startled by the coolness. "Señorita?" he whispered.

"My name is Josefina."

Señor Zamora clutched her arm with unexpected strength. "*Por favor*—where is my sarape?"

"Right over there." Josefina waved her hand toward the pile of clothes. "Don't worry, señor. With God's help, you will soon be well."

His hand fell back to the blanket, and his eyes flickered closed. Josefina touched the damp cloth and found it already warm. She replaced the cloth with another, and Señor Zamora began to murmur again. "The search . . . I must continue my search . . ."

"No, señor," Josefina told him quietly. "Your search for the horse can wait."

His head turned from side to side. "The rock,"

he muttered. "I found the rock."

Josefina bit her lip. "Please, señor," she begged. "Try to rest."

Teresita entered the sala, her quiet calm as comforting as Tía Dolores's brisk efficiency. "Your aunt asked me to sit with him," she told Josefina. "How is he?"

"Not well," Josefina said, regarding their visitor.

Teresita gave Josefina a reassuring smile that lit her whole face. "Don't worry, Señorita Josefina. If God wills it, our guest will recover."

Josefina nodded. She'd done what she could for Señor Zamora.

As she left the sala, she carried his dirty sarape out to the courtyard. It was too late in the day to launder his filthy shirt and trousers, but she could at least shake the dust from his sarape. It had once been of good quality, woven well of yellow and blue and red wool, but Josefina had trouble seeing the pattern through the dirt.

She gripped the woven cloak by the edge and gave it a hard, snapping shake. A cloud of dust billowed into the air. And something white fluttered to the ground.

Josefina stooped to pick up the piece of paper. It

was thin, stained, and tattered. Three sides of the paper were cut straight. The fourth was ragged, as if this piece had come from a larger piece of paper that had been torn in two.

Squinting at the faded ink, Josefina made out an outline that looked familiar: a tall column supporting a flat surface. *That looks like Balancing Rock!* she thought. Was *that* the rock Señor Zamora had been speaking of? She tried to make out the other faint sketches: arrows, a turtle, curved lines that looked like a rainbow.

A burst of conversation from the kitchen interrupted Josefina's study, and her cheeks grew warm. This paper didn't belong to her! Taking a closer look at Señor Zamora's sarape, she found that he had stitched a small piece of thin hide to the inside of the cloak, making a hidden pocket. The map must have fallen from that pocket when she shook the sarape.

Clara appeared at the kitchen door. "Josefina? We're ready for the evening meal."

"Coming!" Josefina called. She slipped the fragile map carefully back into the sarape's hidden pocket, gently brushed what dust she could from the cloak, and folded it in such a way that the pocket—and the map it contained—lay flat. Then she returned the sarape to the sala. She would wash the other clothes tomorrow, and whenever Señor Zamora was ready to be on his way, he would find his map just where he had left it.

But tucking the map away couldn't erase it from Josefina's mind. She remembered their servant Miguel's reaction to the cross scratched into a cave wall: "If God wants me to find buried treasure, I hope He will send me a map!"

Señor Zamora had told Miguel that he'd been searching for a missing mare. Yet his map, old as it was, had surely not been drawn to show him where to look for a horse! He was searching for something else, she was sure of it. Something secret. So . . . what was he seeking?

About the Author

VALERIE TRIPP, the author of *Sunlight and Shadows* and *Second Chances*, says that she became a writer because of the kind of person she is. She says she's curious, and writing requires you to be interested in everything. Talking is her favorite sport, and writing is a way of talking on paper. She's a daydreamer, which helps her come up with her ideas. And she loves words. She even loves the struggle to come up with just the right words as she writes and rewrites. Ms. Tripp lives in Maryland with her husband.

About the Advisory Board

American Girl extends its deepest appreciation
to the advisory board that authenticated Josefina's stories.

Rosalinda B. Barrera, Professor of Curriculum &
Instruction, New Mexico State University, Las Cruces

Juan R. García, Professor of History and Associate Dean
of the College of Social & Behavioral Sciences,
University of Arizona, Tucson

Sandra Jaramillo, Director, Archives & Historical Services,
New Mexico Records Center & Archives, Santa Fe

Skip Keith Miller, Co-director/Curator,
Kit Carson Historic Museums, Taos, NM

Felipe R. Mirabal, former Curator of Collections,
El Rancho de las Golondrinas Living Museum, Santa Fe, NM

Tey Diana Rebolledo, Professor of Spanish,
University of New Mexico, Albuquerque

Orlando Romero, Senior Research Librarian,
Palace of the Governors, Santa Fe, NM

Marc Simmons, Historian, Cerillos, NM